THE YEAR THEY WON

A Tale of the Boston Red Sox

Gerard Purciello

Brown Barn Books
Weston, Connecticut

Brown Barn Books
A division of Pictures of Record, Inc.
119 Kettle Creek Road, Weston, CT 06883, U.S.A.
www.brownbarnbooks.com

THE YEAR THEY WON
Copyright © 2005 by Gerard Purciello

Original paperback edition

Library of Congress Control Number 2004111713

ISBN: 0-974648159

Purciello, Gerard
THE YEAR THEY WON

Printed in the United States of America

DEDICATION

To my Mom, who always told me it's better to play
outside, my Dad, who bought me my first baseball
glove, and my brothers and sisters, who continue
to make me smile . . . this is for you.

And for Uncle Vin, who guided this writer,
and whose sun will forever shine on me.

PROLOGUE

Being a kid was rapid the summer of 2024, knockout rapid.

You could steal a pack of gum, lift a loaf of bread, even fart on purpose in church (not me, Mom), get caught, then in two days all was back to normal inside your special "reserved for kids" bubble. As a kid you had life all figured out, the fine line between escape and capture. And when I tell you we had life figured out, we had it *all* figured out!

We made a circle promise, Lights, Paulie, Capisce, and me, Tags, for as long as we live never to forget that summer of '24. How could we ever?

ONE

A redeeming quality of being a kid is that sometimes you don't realize the consequences of your actions until many years later. Usually you'd never have a clue what consequences meant if it wasn't for an adult telling you what you did was evil, wrong, bad, dumb, downright childish, or irresponsible. And sometimes what you did as a kid finally hits you square in the nose like an overhand right when you find out what the word "consequences" means. You could be watching a movie, riding a bike, daydreaming in school, or you just might be ninety years old when, bam! Right then and there the thought occurs what you did was pretty darn knockout . . . or pretty darn stupid. I'm talking about the Plan.

I say that because we may have stolen the World Series for the city of Boston that summer of 2024. I like to think we tried for all the fans who had been waiting and hoping twenty long years since that glorious October of 2004. Did we succeed? If we didn't, it wasn't for a lack of effort or worry. We most likely just led our lives. I know it was without the thought of consequences. But consequences looming on the horizon or not, I'm positive of two things: four kids grew into men, and the grass we played in was much more important to us than any adult-designated consequences. Nothing would derail what made our summer of 2024 one for the ages.

===

From the beginning of that summer to the polite entrance of the cooling autumn, the one memory I've held over the years is how

1

incredible the grass looked and felt. It was greener than any green I had ever seen. Green decorated our clothes, and the fresh smell of newly cut grass followed us around like skin. And soft? We lounged in it and landed on it while chasing baseballs. We lived in it all summer long. Everything on earth smelled of this sweet color, and because of it, everything was perfect.

And the sky? I can't begin to explain to you how high and blue the sky was that endless summer except to say many of our fly balls and pop-ups dropped untouched because the sky devoured the baseball. The ball would go up and up and up, transformed into a tiny dark speck against the sky, and then drop like a heavy white snowflake wherever we weren't. The trees were full with more fruit than a world could eat. We snacked on deep-red cherries like a murder of crows pecking from the trees. And when we got sick of cherries, we hit the pear trees or apple trees.

Nothing intruded on that summer. Not death, not illness, not untimely family vacations. I don't recall a grownup yelling at us in anger or even a dog barking at a mailman. Returning to school in September never became a topic. It was baseball, baseball and more baseball. From early morning to late afternoon, the four of us, four of the happiest souls in the entire universe, played, talked, and dreamed baseball.

We were all twelve years old: Joe "Lights" Beacon and his twin brother Paul "Paulie"; Peter "Capisce" Capiscio and me, Jerry "Tags" Taglia. The weight of the world wasn't on our young minds just yet. Not what we were going to do with our lives or how much money we were going to make. Not what car we were going to drive or where we were going to live. And none of us were talking seriously about girls, not yet, anyway. Nothing mattered except one thing; the Boston Red Sox, our Boston Red Sox were about to win—*again,* I emphasize—the World Series again for the first time in twenty years.

No one who grew up outside of New England can look us long-suffering loyalists in the face and tell us they remotely understand the significance of the prospect of another eighty-six years of losing baseball. It was now twenty years of great players being sold, players holding the ball too long, umpires making rotten calls, managers and coaches making bad decisions, and balls going between players' legs. Those eighty-six years between 1918 and 2004, the last time they won, were tattooed on every Red Sox fan's forehead as a symbol of failure and a reminder to every city that enjoyed our failure for the past twenty years. This Old Towne Team's futility since 2004 cut at our city like a razor.

We heard from our great-grandmothers and -fathers and parents how they had suffered but endured the endless "almost" and "wait-'til-next -year" litanies. And the players who for eighty-six years gave their all, came to camp in March with hope, only to leave in October with aches and plenty of opportunity to heal over the winter. It was now twenty years of again turning the best baseball players into a combination of the Three Stooges and Spanky and the Our Gang kids when the chips were on the table.

But not that year! In 2024 we were finally going to do laps at midnight and storm the castle and take no prisoners and drink from the cup until we passed out for weeks. We were going to do the things that all happened before we were even born. Boston was going to win the World Series again in 2024, because Lights, Paulie, Capisce, and me, Tags, four sawed-off snot-nosed Red Sox bleeding kids from tiny Belmont, Massachusetts, were going to steal it for them. We were going to march into Fenway Park (the old Fenway Park, that is; the city built a new ballpark but nobody came, so they reopened the old one, with the old net above the Green Monster), and steal the deciding game that would once again bring the city the World Series and make us heroes forever. Our goal was to stop the Curse from descending on Boston again, so our names would forever be linked to the greats that gave to the deserving. I imagined myself as Robin Hood with my best friends my band of brothers, stealing from the Evil Yankee Kingdom and giving back to the fans of tiny Bostontown the glory they had tasted twenty years before.

So the Plan was set, and I've got to say, not necessarily because it was my idea, but the Plan, like the blue sky, the summer weather, the hours upon hours of baseball nirvana, and the green grass that glorious summer of 2024, *was* perfect!

TWO

Outside it was seventy-five degrees and flawless as usual. I could smell fresh cut grass as if I had slept in it last night. I went to my open window and breathed in the freedoms of summer. Could anything be so right as right now? Maybe just one thing would improve my early morning. I glanced through the branches of our cherry tree for a glimpse of my next door neighbor, Mrs. Emory, who once had her picture in a girly magazine as Miss April, doing just about anything inside her house. Sometimes I got lucky, but this morning I struck out. It didn't bother me though—I had other more important things to occupy me.

The Red Sox were in first place, a ten-game lead over the disgusting inbreds from New York, the New Yawk Jan-keys, as Capisce liked to say. Ten games ahead on July 10th, the first game of the second half of the season—even our beloved nine couldn't lose this much of a lead again. I sat on the edge of my bed and glanced at the posters on my wall. They were tacked up in a diamond shape, my shrine to The Best Darn Baseball Team in the Universe. First base, Bo Henry; second, Hal Wallace; short, Lee Lozaino; third, Tony Palagrini; left, Hilberto Otto; center Stanley Dupree; right, Grady Telinger; catching, Steve Berano; and pitching, "The Right-handed Rifleman," Kurt Winchester (rumor had it that he was cloned from Roger Clemens, or at least that's what Mr. Capiscio believed).

Over them all in full classic swing, was the forty-year-old kid, Louie Cardinale. I got off my bed and got into full Cardinale mode.

I tugged at my imaginary helmet, pulled on my elbow wrap, nudged at my batting gloves, right hand over left, left under right, three times, stepped into the batter's box and toed the dirt until the pitcher was ready. First pitch was a flat fastball and I sent it screaming into the net and over the Green Monster.

"You da man, L.C.!"

I high-fived my teammates, who mobbed me as I crossed home plate, and pulled out my statistics book from under the bed to look up his numbers: .325 average, sixteen homers, fifty runs batted in, and that was at the All-Star break. I closed my book and laughed at those (my dad, and most of my friend's dads) who said Cardinale was too old and couldn't hit the fastball any longer. I repeated by memory—lifetime .326 batting average, five hundred and five homers, 1,950 rbi. Too old? The guy could hit a fastball blindfolded. And he still had the speed to leg out a wall double or go from first to third on a single.

They were going to win the Series this year, not just come close like in '09, when an injured L.C. had to limp to the plate with a gimpy knee and try like the warrior he is to smack one out. They were so close that year, my dad told me. With the winning run on first, two outs and trailing by one against the Cardinals, the Sox had Tiny Zuleski, the Olympic speedster on first. All he had to do was reach home plate before L.C. was thrown out at first base.

But as Red Sox fate would have it, L.C. ripped a base hit and twisted his knee getting out of the batter's box and had to crawl toward first base as the right fielder gathered the ball and threw him out at first, a second before Tiny Zuleski, the fastest human alive, hit home plate. They lost the game and the series, and all of Boston shook their heads in exasperation.

They were going to win this year because Louie Cardinale, or L.C., was going to carry them on his back if needed. (We hadn't put together my Plan just yet). He was going to win it for the '06 team of W. Pollack and Tommy Front. The '15 team of G.E. Tamirez and Yancy Rodriguez. But mostly he was going to win for the '24 team of Bo Henry, Hilberto Otto, and the Rifleman, Kurt Winchester.

"Tags, you up?" Lights Beacon's voice drifted up to my second-story bedroom window. "Tags, Tags?"

One thing about Lights you'll discover, he's sort of the nervous, impatient type, but in an okay way. I slid the book back under my bed and took another swing for L.C., dead center field, a 410-foot bomb that kept traveling up, up, and "tell-it-so-long-everybody." I pumped my fist and waved to the shrieking crowd.

"Tags, we're waitin' on you. Tags?"

I poked my head out the window. "Lights, relax, son. I hear you. Give me fifteen minutes and I'll meet you at your house. Capisce there already?" I knew he was. You could set your watch on Capisce showing up at the Beacons' doorstep by eight every morning.

"What do you think? He showed up this morning eating a bowl of cereal . . . and get this, he had the milk and box of cereal with him. He was just sittin' eatin' away when I opened the back door." Lights pretended he was shoveling food into his mouth.

"Get out! The guy's whacked." I threw a tiny plastic Robo Man out my window at Lights. "I'll see you at your house. Oh, and Lights? Tell-it-so-long everrryhboddy."

Lights repeated his best (which actually was the worst I've ever heard) Downtown Davey Higgins, the radio voice of the Boston Red Sox, do his patented home run call. "Tell it sooooo long everybody!" He made the noise of the crowd cheering. Then he lowered his voice. "Tags? Is Mrs. Emory up?"

"Only for me."

"Yeah, you wish." He gave me a Bronx cheer and trotted off.

I actually did wish, as in, really, really wish. I stepped around the clutter on the bedroom floor and remembered Mom told me two days ago to clean up the room. Tonight, definitely tonight, I'd tell her. I pushed most of the stuff—my shirts, socks, and a couple of baseball magazines—under the bed. My whackanut cat, Twotails, hissed and jumped down the other side of my bed. My computer screen was still glowing from forgetting to shut it off last night; a Red Sox screen saver floated in psychedelic reds, whites, and blues around and through a baseball diamond. As computer geeks go, I was on the bottom rung. I knew how they worked, what made them work, and sometimes why they didn't work, but my interest stopped there. Since I could remember, I preferred to be on the baseball field than in some cyber-cooked-up 3D-generated field. I flipped the off switch on the monitor and the Red Sox emblem faded out.

"Come on, Twotails, you coming this mornin?" Of course the cat was coming. She followed me around like a piece of toilet paper stuck to the bottom of my shoe. My friends liked to kid me about it because they never saw a cat following a person around like a dog would their owner. To tell you the truth, I never did either, but I thought it was kind of rapid. She came around the back of the bed and stopped at my leg to rub and purr. I patted her on the bum and laughed. Old Twotails had no tail, don't know if she ever had. The guys and I found her roaming around the bushes where we play, her black fur all matted and her white socks dirty, and figured, what better name for a homeless cat with no tail than Twotails. The Beacons' father wouldn't allow an animal, and the Capiscios had a dog, so Twotails became mine, against the expected Mom and Dad Better Judgement argument. But old Twotails won them over, and she could stay as long as I fed her and groomed her . . . well, one out of two ain't bad.

I pulled off my button-down nightshirt and tossed it under the bed, adding to the growing pile, and bounded toward the bathroom, but not before stopping at the dresser mirror to flex my arms. I was building some major-league muscles. Ninety-one pounds now, five-feet, three inches tall, a tough-guy short haircut. I looked closely into the mirror—no stubble growing just yet, only a new red pimple on my cheek. I was feeling powerful nonetheless . . . I was L.C. I threw a handful of water over my face and brushed my teeth. Today was going to be a "get-at-it-day," I could feel it. One of those days when my dad liked to think that nothing could or would ruin the great feeling of being alive. My dad being a button salesman, I couldn't fathom that selling buttons could make anyone feel like busting out of bed and hitting the road with both legs motoring. But he did, and I could always tell if it had been a "get-at-it-day" when he came home at night.

In my world, a good "get-at-it-day" meant I went two-for-four, extra-base hit, maybe knocked in a run, and played error-free ball in the field. I'd had a lot of those. A bad "get-at-it-day" was an oh-for-four, couple of strikeouts, throw in an error. I'd had a few of those, too. But a real, genuine, bona fide, look-at-me-world, "get-at-it-day," was a four-for-four, two home runs, and dazzling defense. Dad had a few of those days thrown in, but I doubt enough to make the Button Hall of Fame.

I grabbed my new glove from under the mattress and untied the shoelace that held it tight. Dad did have a great "get-at-it-day" one day last week, and after dinner, he couldn't wait to walk me out to his car. There in a box on his front car seat was a new Louie Cardinale Special Issue shortstop glove. You could smell the leather the minute my dad opened the car door; it was as if the glove were dripping leather syrup. It was sleek, the most perfect black rawhide glove I had ever seen. On the finger in large white letters were Louie Cardinale's initials, L.C. in script. The web seemed to go on forever when I slipped it on my hand. I'd be able to catch a sleeping baby from a burning skyscraper with this thing and not wake up the kid. See you later, minor leagues, I laughed. I had just moved up to the majors.

"Smother the glove in baby oil. I'll get some from your mother," Dad told me. "Then get a baseball, put it inside the web and tie it really tight with a shoelace. Then slip it under your mattress when you go to sleep. The oil will soften it and it will fold much easier when you catch the ball. And don't forget to put your name on it."

After he gave me the glove, I promised him that for the rest of my life in his honor I'd always buy buttondown shirts. I slept with the glove under my mattress for two weeks, only taking it out to flex it and oil it more before placing it back. That glove was so darn soft, it felt like a wet flower petal.

"Give it two weeks," Dad had promised, "and you should be able to catch a no-see-um."

I thanked him so many times he told me "enough already" before I skipped off, looking for no-see-ums and wishing Dad sold baseball stuff instead of dopey buttons.

Today, the first day of the second half of the season, was the day. Today the glove got unveiled. I knew the guys were going to flip when they saw how beautiful it was. I looked up one more time while slipping my Rifleman's (only because I was pitching today) white, number 18 Red Sox shirt (buttoned, of course) over my head, at the lineup of Sox. With my Red Sox cleats in hand, Sox socks pulled up to my knees, Sox shorts on straight, and my Sox cap, the white one with the dark blue B and dark blue bill, fitting snugly, I kissed the L.C. glove and inhaled the smell of leather and oil. I almost wished I could eat the glove. It was a "get-at-it-day" for sure.

THREE

Capisce was sitting on the back stairs of the Beacons' house when I walked up. His way-too-big black baseball bat was leaning against the porch. The bat could've been holding the porch up it was that thick. Capisce could hardly grip it. Forget me, my hands couldn't cover half the handle, but no one tried telling Capisce that he should try a smaller-sized bat. He used the thick-grip, thirty-four-ounce Black Python because Hilberto Otto, the Sox left fielder, used one. In fact, it was a "genuine" Otto Black Python. It was definitely a sharp-looking bat, but it was way too big. The empty cereal bowl and box were placed on the step between his knees. I couldn't help notice the cereal was Life and thought, how right on.

Capisce was dressed like me—Sox hat, Sox shirt, Sox pants and Sox socks. He wore Otto's white number 35. Well, it had started out white. It looked as if it hadn't been washed in weeks.

"Hey, Tags, you know who's pitchin' tonight for the . . ." and he stopped talking liked he had just seen a ghost. What he saw was my glove. "Whoa, get out. Where'd ya get that? Let me see it, c'mon, Tags, let me see it. That's wild, oh man! That's knockout." Capisce's huge hand was practically ripping it off my hand.

"Easy, Capisce. Jeez, wait a second." I turned sideways so he wouldn't rip my hand off with the glove.

"Knockout!"

You should know that though Peter "Capisce" Capiscio was twelve, he was as big as a sixteen-year-old. He was a foot taller and had at least a hundred pounds on me and the Beacons, and sometimes he didn't realize just how much stronger he was than us. . . matter of fact, most of the time. I looked up at his square face with deep-set black eyes, and chin that somehow already had early morning stubble, and got scared to death. With his army buzz cut and dark Italian skin, darker than normal because of a summer tan, he reminded me of a black bear—who happened to be ripping my arm off. I thought briefly of running home to Mom. We did a circle dance with Capisce hanging onto my glove.

"Capisce," I pleaded, "if you let go, I'll show you. But you gotta let go. Pleeeeeeeze!"

I thought briefly of kicking him in the shins. A learning show I saw said if you ever get attacked by a bear you're supposed to bat it on its ears and it will freeze. But just then, as Capisce and I did my arm-detachment dance, Paulie and his twin brother Lights came out their back door. I think they saved my arm, or my life if I had kicked Capisce. They also wore their complete Red Sox outfits, Paulie, the blue Rifleman jersey, Lights, the blue Louie Cardinale. Both wore their blue caps with white Bs stitched on the cap.

"Hey Lights, look, the dance of the fairies." Paulie laughed like a little girl, but I was thankful for it at the moment because the giggle caught Capisce's attention.

"Listen to you, calling me a fairy with that laugh." Capisce let go of my glove and pointed at it. "Look what Tags got, guys. It's knockout."

"Wow, knockout!" One voice came from two mouths.

Paulie dropped his bat and glove on the porch and bounded down the four steps in one move. "That is extremely, extremely knockout. Can I see it?"

"I get to see it first." Capisce pointed at Paulie.

"When can I see? I want to see it, too." Lights took the four steps one at a time.

"You'll see it after I see it." Capisce meant it.

I couldn't take it anymore. I thought of running home and climbing underneath my bed with the pile of junk and dirty clothes. Then I remembered it was a "get-at-it-day."

"Okay, you guys just stop right where you are or nobody is gonna see it . . . n-o-b-o-d-y." I immediately felt stupid for spelling "nobody," but it seemed to work. They all came forward but gave me a couple of feet of space. Twotails lay in front of me like she was my bodyguard. "This is how we'll do it." I held the glove behind my back. "'Cause Capisce was here first," and because he was huge and could pop me like a grape, I added, "he sees it first."

Capisce whacked me on the shoulder, almost knocking me on my seat.

"Tags!" Capisce looked at the guys proud as a peacock.

"But," I continued, "only for a minute . . . then Paulie, then Lights."

"Why does Paulie get to see it before me?" Lights looked at me as if I had stolen his bike.

"Because he's older," Capisce answered for me, already reaching around my back for the glove.

"Older? Yeah, by a minute, maybe."

"Older's older, little bro." Paulie stuck his finger in his brother's ear just as Capisce yanked my glove free.

"Take it easy, Capisce, it's brand new." I looked at Capisce and my glove—it just about fit on his hand. He was pounding the leather like you'd hit a punching bag. "Knockout, Tags. Where'd ya get it? The sports store at the mall?"

"Yeah. Easy with it, Capisce. I want to use it before you ruin it."

"How much? Look, L.C.'s name, very knockout." He pounded it. "Huh, how much?"

"Yeah, how much?" The twins were one again.

The fact was, I didn't have a clue. I couldn't tell them my dad bought it because they'd tease me and call me names. I had never ever asked Dad where he bought it. I couldn't have cared less.

"More than you bums can afford." I gave myself an A for alright! "Okay, it's Paulie's turn." Capisce went back as if he was catching a long fly, then flipped it to Paulie.

Just to put me in my place, Capisce added, "You got no excuses now missing flies or grounders with that thing." He patted me on the back and smiled.

We were a team today.

When we started playing every day two years ago, it was Capisce and me against the twins. Since then, I've charted every day who would be teamed with who and constantly rotated the teams.

Sunday, it was me and Paulie. Monday, Capisce and me. Tuesday, Lights and I were teammates. Yesterday, it was Paulie again. Today, Capisce was my teammate. It kept things fair. I didn't mind playing with Capisce; if he could get the Black Python on the ball, he'd hit it a country mile. And there was the problem. He couldn't hit for beans. If I tied a bat to Twotails' paw, she could hit the ball better than Capisce, who was at this moment rolling around with Twotails in the dirt and dust of the Beacons' back yard. However, the guy could catch. Somehow the big guy was given a pair of hands as soft as L.C.'s. And he could run, too. He looked very silly when he did, sort of like a cowboy who had just climbed off a horse, all bow-legged and stiff. But it worked. We all stopped making fun of him after the first month of playing together because we all saw he could catch knockout. When we were teamed, we would also switch who pitched. Today I was throwing the pea; today I was the Rifleman.

The twins were finished tossing the new glove around, Capisce and Twotails were finished rolling in the dirt, and I wanted to get on the field to use my new glove. We headed to the Pit, our home away from home, and the world in the palm of our hand.

Lights pointed at the Python. "Don't forget your sweetheart, Capisce. Smoochie, smoochie!" Lights didn't hesitate; he took off running down the street with Capisce flying behind him growling like a mad dog. I lightly punched Paulie in the arm and he punched back as we followed them, alternating punches and laughing. Watching Capisce running bowlegged after Lights gave me stomach pains I never thought I'd welcome.

FOUR

The Pit was fifteen minutes from the Beacons' house if you walked our summer-no-hurry stroll, which the four of us swore we invented. By cutting through the town's closed elementary school parking lot and then down the never-used playground hill, the Pit was located in what the old-timers called, the "worn" part of town, the section of town that had given way to urban development on the other side of Belmont. Not one of us understood what the heck that even meant. All we knew was that the town decided to leave the "worn" part, and just for us.

Once we were at the bottom of the playground, we slipped through a broken section of wooden fence that was also the boundary line of the town's ancient dump. The dump hadn't been used in years. In fact, my dad told me that for the past fifteen years, trash had been shot out into space because we have no more room left on this planet to put it, so we drop it off on planets around us.

Everything in the dump was rusted, including the shed we used as our dugout when it rained. The aged shed still had a pot-bellied stove and a table with chairs when we'd found it over three years ago . . . and a couple of old girly magazines that helped keep our interest during rain delays. Which wasn't often this year (which was a good thing for Lights, because he'd turn so beet red when he looked at the pictures, we thought he was going to explode). The shed was only about as big as a bathroom, and the roof leaked some, but it kept us dry and was sort of our treehouse on the ground. Plus, we just had to find it, not build it ourselves. When we passed the shed, we'd turn left past the old milk delivery truck and over a pile of tires, then crawl under another wooden fence that bordered the dump. On the other side of the creaky fence was our Fenway Park.

As I proudly stood and looked at our diamond, the field in that old movie, Field of Dreams, always entered my mind. That one had lush green grass, rich, brown-dirt base paths, a regulation pitching mound and six-foot-high corn stalks surrounding the entire field. Our field had a few minor differences. We did have to walk through a field to get there, but it wasn't a cornfield, it was a fly-infested dump. Old cars, refrigerators, dryers, washing machines and every imaginable nut, bolt and screw was our cornfield.

The playing area was a square and only about sixty by sixty. It had worn-down black dirt with scrubby patches of grass. The pitching mound was a spot marked off by twenty large paces from home plate and had a brick dug into it that was the pitching rubber.

Home plate and the bases were hubcaps buried in the ground thirty steps from home. Behind home plate was the wooden fence that worked as the backstop. The creaky old fence extended to right field and left. If the ball was hit foul to the right or left, we could retrieve it in the dump. But if we hit one over the right-field treeline, the ball would land in the dirty stillwater hole we had named the Pit. If you could hit one there, the game was called on account of having no ball to play with because it would be sucked into the dead water.

The trees on the right were high and thick, and you really had to get under the ball to knock it high enough and over. None of us batted left-handed, so it rarely happened. Miraculously, Capisce was the only one since we started playing to hit a ball into the Pit— twice, as a matter of fact— so we never even concerned ourselves with it. We were more concerned about pulling the ball, turning on one just like our heroes, and tagging one deep into left field and into the net above . . . The Green Monster.

Sixty feet away from home plate loomed the back wall of an old abandoned warehouse. A dairy farm in its day, the walls were red brick and solid, higher than the trees in right. The wall even had a door, bricked over now, but like the door on the actual Green Monster.

We figured it must've been the door the cows walked through to graze in this yard. The Green Monster (Mr. Capiscio owned a hardware store so we "borrowed" all the green paint we needed and touched it up) started on the fence line of the dump and went beyond centerfield. The wall must've been fifty feet high. And because it was close to home plate, we couldn't actually jack one over the wall—not even Capisce when he hit the ball. So we invented our own net, just like the one on top of The Green Monster. We found three battered but usable extendable aluminum ladders in the dump. We placed one against the wall down the left-field line, and leaned one against the wall we called centerfield. We extended the ladders as high as they could go, about twenty feet, and we tied a clothesline across the tops, and another from a step about ten rungs lower. We found enough chicken wire and fence wire to feed the clothesline through to make the net. When the ladders were angled from the wall, a ball hit into the net would stay just like a home run hit at Fenway. We used the other ladder when we had to retrieve the ball from the net.

The field was a dream to us. No one could see us, we were tucked away secure and happy. And now, as I looked over at our diamond, all the blood in my veins pumped like it was the first time I stepped on the field. I figured it must've been the way Louie Cardinale felt stepping onto his Fenway Park.

Lights, Paulie and I stood on the third-base line and removed our hats. Capisce could barely fit under the fence, so he always went last. When he popped through, we stood in a perfect line. Twotails was already rolling in the pitcher's mound dirt. The sun wasn't at its full height yet, so shadows were painted on the wall in left. I shivered with excitement; I sensed a knockout day in the making.

I squinted and studied the big left-field wall. Sometimes birds got tangled in the net and it was our duty to free them before singing our national anthem. The net was free of birds today. I rubbed my eyes and held my hat over my heart. We sang the anthem out of key, and then we yelled in key, "Play ball!" and moved to home plate.

"Who calls? Paulie?" I asked.

"I'll call."

"You called last time. Let me call," Lights whined.

"Every time you call, we end up being the visiting team." Paulie stepped in front of his brother to face me.

I held the quarter on the edge of my finger, ready to flip to decide which team batted first or last. According to my charts, Paulie and Lights called the flip today. Not according to my charts —I should've kept track of it—was the surefire argument this always started.

"That's not always true. C'mon, let me call." Lights tried to push Paulie aside. Although they were identical twins, brown hair, brown eyes and the same height, about five feet tall, Paulie was ten pounds heavier. Paulie probably weighed the same as me. He didn't move much when shoved.

I stood patiently, but Capisce was starting to snort.

"Go ahead, Tags, flip it." Paulie kept Lights aside.

I flipped the coin.

"Heads," he called.

Lights complained some more and knocked Paulie's cap off, but we all watched in silence as the quarter did a sun-splashed flip; it landed off the home-plate hubcap. Heads.

"Ha, I'm the man." Paulie strutted to the mound as Lights kicked him lightly in the rear as he passed him. "You make any errors and you're a dead man."

"I won't, just don't give up any gophers either." Lights got in position under the Green Monster.

I yelled out to Lights, "What time does L.C. say it is?" Lights had a wristwatch of L.C. taking a full swing in its center, his back with the number five facing you. When you pushed in a tiny button on the side of the watch, the sound of a bat cracking a ball and the crowd roaring would begin, then you'd hear Louie Cardinale's voice reading the time.

"It's 8:43, AM . . . L.C. time."

We all laughed. When twelve o'clock struck, it was the greatest—the crack of the bat, the roar of the crowd, then L.C.'s voice.

Then, a little Louie Cardinale would pop out above the six and scamper around the clock like he was running out a home run while the crowd roared. It was knockout.

"We break at twelve for lunch, right?" We'd be home before twelve-thirty and back on the field an hour later.

"Twelve it is." Paulie was warming up with Capisce catching.

The rules of the game were simple. We used only wooden bats, no aluminum. Because a hard ball traveled farther and was more expensive, you could crush a tennis ball out of town, and a Wiffle ball too light for the wooden bat, we used a modified Wiffle ball. I figured this out. You take a Wiffle ball and wrap white cloth tape around it three times, but no more. It gives the ball just enough weight but not so much that it shoots out of the park.

There were no walks, and if a batter hit three consecutive foul balls, he was out on a strikeout. If a ground ball didn't make it out of the infield, it was an out. If a hit ball passed the outfielder and rolled to the wall in either left or center, it was a single. Right field was an out, except if you hit it over the trees; then it was a home run. A double was a hit on one bounce or straight off the wall. A triple was a hit above a line we'd drawn that was just below the net in left. There was no base-running, except if you hit a home run, then you could "style" running around the bases. Most of us liked to run out a hit just to keep the feel of the game. If there was a runner on first, he could only advance to third on a double. A runner on third scored on a single, but a runner on second only advanced one base on a single. A double scored the runner from second base. There were three outs a team and nine innings a game.

We kept the score with chalk on a scoreboard we'd painted made to look like the scoreboard on the left-field wall at Fenway. We had fine-tuned the old rules a little over the years, trying to speed up the game and keep it more like a baseball score than a football score. Before these new rules, a lot of games would never end. We'd be finishing in the dark and running home late for dinner.

We all agreed on one improvement, and I was working on that.

FIVE

Mom was nuking dinner when I skipped through the door. I stopped only long enough to drink a glass of lemonade before Lights was at my screen door.

"Hey Tags. Tags? You gonna watch the game here or at my house?"

His voice was straining to hold in our secret. I opened the door just wide enough to allow Twotails to slip in, looking like a gray dirt ball with yellow eyes. She walked past me, and clouds of dust floated off her. Lights wanted to come in, but I knew my mother would be setting the table soon and I also had just spent the whole day with him.

"Go home and eat, Lights. I'll call you later, okay? And keep quiet about tonight."

I closed the door and could hear his voice on the other side. He was going to give our plan away, plus, he wanted to soak up their win today . . . that's what he really wanted to do. A last-inning double by Paulie scored their winning run. That was okay, though, the winning team always won with very little dignity.

"Good game, huh, Tags?" He was leaving, but not before one last hit. Yeah, it actually had been good, but no way I was letting on. I turned around and saw Mom.

"Go wash up. Your father'll be home any minute." She was moving around the kitchen like a bumblebee, so I dodged her and headed upstairs to wash off the caked dirt and the sweet smell of a "get-at-it-day." Although our team lost, it hadn't ruined the feel of what we lived for. I still had my glove hanging from my wrist when I sat on the side of my bed. I took off the glove and held it warmly in my lap, wondering if it would ever look and smell so good as it did right now. Even the little bit of dirt smeared over the web looked as if it belonged. I held it high and relived the line drive off Paulie's bat; the ball had come at me like a missile, rising from the ground and shooting over my head like a bottlerocket. But at the last second (and with my eyes closed, which I'll never tell the guys), I flipped the glove above my head and started running toward the wall. Somehow, miraculously, the webbing of my glove seemed to call the ball into its soft center. I heard it settle into the new leather as softly as a falling cherry. It was one of those catches that has a moment of silence before everyone breaks out in their best "Get lost!" "No way!" "You gotta-be-kidding!" All the guys thought it was my new glove. I had to agree, but no way I was going to admit it. I tossed the ball back like I'd been catching those for years.

I patted the glove like I would Twotails. I knew how new things got old quickly; my father's new car lost that new-car smell in two weeks, and Mom's laptop computer after two weeks became buried under a foot of newspapers and magazines. I couldn't stop staring at the glove and wondering if it would it shrink when I grew. Dad once told me that the house he grew up in shrunk, and the mountain he used to climb over as a kid was really a rock no taller than he was today. I suppose these things happen when a kid becomes an adult. But how could my glove shrink? Maybe things shrank when you didn't care about them any longer? I folded the glove and put it on my dresser, glad to have it safely home, and made a cross-my-heart-and-hope-to-die promise I'd never allow it to get old . . . at least not before I did.

I sat patiently at the kitchen table waiting for the right moment to excuse myself. I loved my parents, but it was torture to have to sit here after eating and listen to their stories of another day at the office. I mean, Mom sitting downstairs in the cellar putting buttons in plastic zip-lock bags all day didn't exactly make for a thrilling pastime. And selling the buttons? Well, you can only imagine.

Dad did have a pretty good get-at-it-day. Some big-time owner of a boat building company bought a zillion buttons, so I listened thinking, just maybe, a new bat might be in the works. I had no brothers or sisters so I guess it was my job to keep my parents company.

"May I be excused?" Dad's story of the boat's cushions needing new green-blue button to match the color of the hull had ended, so I muscled in.

"You watching the game here tonight or at the boys' house?" Mom needed to know what I was doing every minute of the day. "Did you clean your room like I asked you?"

Oh no, forgot again. "We're going to the Beacons' house. Oh, by the way, Dad, the glove was knockout, caught everything that was hit to me." I pretended to pick a grounder up and toss the ball. I wanted to tell him about the incredible catch but decided that another time would be better so I could let it grow a little.

"Excellent. Did you oil it?"

"Gonna do that now." I took my empty plate to the new Cleanerama and slipped it onto the conveyor. The glass and utensils I put in special pockets beside the dish. Watching through a clear glass window, I turned the switch on and stepped closer; the dish was first scraped clean by a rubber arm then shoved into a furnace. The plate was tipped sideways and four lights flashed on the dirty stuff. I loved looking directly at flash of light (of course against Mom's constant warnings); the light would make my eyes goofy for a couple of minutes, and I could imagine there were dancing animals in front of me. Sounds stupid, but actually it was knockout.

Dad had told me that the flash was a low-intensity nuclear blast intended to fry the germs. He said it was also intended to save our planet's water which was dangerously low. It was pretty much outlawed for families to use between certain hours. That was all adult stuff anyway, their worries; it was tough enough to be a kid. Once the dishes, glass and utensils were fried, they were dropped out a door and onto a soft cushion and then moved out of the way of other dishes. It doesn't seem like much, I know, but the Cleanerama was new so I hadn't gotten used to it yet. I put the clean plate, glass and utensils away. I wondered if my glove became really dirty a blast of the Cleanerama would come in handy. I'd have to ask Dad.

"Clean your room, young man, before you go out," Mom said. "Who's home at the Beacons'? I don't want you over there without adult supervision."

"Their parents will be home." I had no idea if they would be, but Mom wouldn't know. I was itching to get out because tonight we had other plans.

"I'll clean my room now." I ran upstairs, eager to get going and get the Plan ironed out before I told the guys. I pulled the pile of clothes out from under the bed and spread them out around the room while Twotails tried to tackle my shoelaces. I piled the dirty shirts going in the wash against the door. The books and stat sheets I stacked and slid neatly against the wall under the head of my bed, just in case I needed to check a stat quickly. I emptied Twotails' water bowl and tossed it on the pile of clothes that was on the way downstairs to the washing machine. I scooped up all the plastic dinosaurs, army men, baseball players and cards and threw them into the treasure chest at the foot of my bed. The whole ordeal took ten minutes.

Seated again, I checked the Red Sox schedule. The team was home tonight, and for the next ten games. I shook with excitement. This was going to be so knockout!

=

"We're gonna get killed, I just know it." Lights shook his head and whispered as if his cellar were bugged by the Parent Police Force. He kept looking up the stairs, expecting his parents to come busting down.

"Oh, stop your whining, Lights. You're the one who was all psyched up and everything earlier. It'll work knockout, isn't that right, Tags?"

Capisce looked across the room at me with a little doubt in his face. It made me feel better that even a guy his size could be afraid. "Tell him no problem, mook. And it's the Jan-keys, man, the stinkin' Jan-keys."

"Absolutely none," I made the mark of an "x" across my chest, "or hope to die."

"I dunno. What if we don't make it back in time? Paulie and I will be grounded for the summer." Lights kept watching the stairs.

Paulie was sitting on the couch, tossing a ball in the air, playing catch by himself. "We won't, Lights. Listen to Tags. We go in, stay four innings, and we're home by nine o'clock. Nobody will know. We're in and out like bank robbers."

Yeah, I thought, in and out like bank robbers.

"Just one question, Tags. How we gonna get into the ballpark?" Capisce snatched away the ball right before it landed in Paulie's hand and peered at me. "Ya know . . . in."

I looked at him and realized I hadn't thought of that little problem.

"Well, that's the secret." I scratched my chin, stalling for a few seconds to come up with an idea that sounded strong. Truth was, I really hadn't thought of actually sneaking into Fenway. The idea of sneaking off to Fenway was rapid enough. "You guys let me worry about getting in. I know what I'm doin'."

My dad told me once of a guy who had snuck into the button factory (why, I don't have any idea) by crawling down a manhole in the street, then up a drain pipe that happened to be inside their parking garage. Sounded rapid, except I hadn't a clue if Fenway had a garage like that. I guess we were about to find out.

We told our folks we were walking to Belmont Center to have an ice cream cone and promised we'd be back by nine o'clock. We had Lights' and Paulie's parents' permission to tent out in the Beacons' backyard because Mrs. and Mr. Beacon were going out and wouldn't be home until ten. So if we slipped up a little, at least we'd have some time to cover our butts. I didn't want to think about that, though. We had the whole summer ahead, so screwing up would be a big-league error.

We all had our gloves with us just in case of foul balls. I know we were being really optimistic on that aspect, but Capisce thought even if we didn't sneak inside, we'd hang out behind the Green Monster and hope for a home run that cleared the net above the wall. So we all split for home to grab our gloves and then meet back at the Beacons' house. I grabbed a bag of beef jerky from the pantry, scooped a tennis ball just to throw around as we walked the tracks, and scooted out the back door with Twotails practically sewn to my ankle.

"My parents just left." Paulie and Lights were setting up the tent just as Twotails, Capisce, and I rounded the corner.

"I got a good idea. I have to ditch Twotails somewhere. She can't be following us. We gotta hurry though—we've got about an hour to get there. The bigger the crowd, the better it is to sneak inside."

We each grabbed an end of the tent and had the corners tied down in minutes. I tossed the cat inside and zipped the flap before she knew what was happening.

We bolted down Orchard Street and crossed Concord Avenue. We ran across Belmont High School's football field and slipped through the chain-link fence that separated the high school from the Boston-to-Maine train tracks.

The four of us were on the tracks and heading toward Fenway in less than fifteen minutes. It wasn't the fastest way to Fenway and definitely not the best, but the alternative wasn't anything any of us would ever agree upon, not in a million years, and only then in an emergency—Ratso's tunnel.

"Who's pitchin' for the Jan-keys, I mean the sis-sies?" Lights pounded his brother's back for approval; he liked his own joke. Paulie flicked the back of Lights' ear with his finger, but you could see Paulie sort of liked his brother's joke. As unrapid as it was to like anything of his brother's, right now it was rapid because everything was rapid. I passed around the beef jerky.

"Yeah, the sis-sies. Gotta like it." Capisce pretended to be fielding ground balls as he walked the tracks.

I flipped the tennis ball over my shoulder and he nabbed it without looking; the kid did have some sweet hands. I looked the length of the railroad tracks and watched the heat rise from the metal rails. I absolutely, positively loved this time of year.

"Don't go near Ratso's hole," I teased Lights.

"Don't have to worry about that," they answered as one.

"Ask Tags, he knows the starting rotation by heart. Don't you, stat man?"

"By memory, Paulie."

We forgot about the creature known as Ratso for the moment.

"Rooney's hurlin' tonight. Against . . ." I made a noise with my mouth like I was cocking a rifle. I lifted the rifle to my eye and pulled the trigger. "Pow, the Rifleman, Kurt Winchester, on the mound tonight."

"Oh, man, knock-knock-knockout! What a game this is gonna be!"

"Knockout!"

"Definitely knockout."

I finished our agreement, "GET-OUT-OF-HERE KNOCKOUT!" Which was kind of like the cherry on the cake, but I couldn't help myself.

"Rooney, two-point three-five earned run average, eight wins and only one loss; opposing batters are hittin' two twenty-five against him. The Rifleman, one point seven-eight earned run average, eleven wins and NO, thank you very much, l-o-s-s-e-s. Opposing batters hittin' just one ninety-eight against him, but only one thirty-one at home. How's that, girls?"

We located the hole in the fence between two warehouses and ran off the tracks and down the worn path onto Brookline Avenue and Kenmore Square. Fenway was one big party. People were cutting in and out between other people, cars were dodging in and around other cars and people, kids were being dragged along by their parents, vendors were yelling, "hot dogs!" "sausages!" "peanuts!" "popcorn!" "hats!" "programs!" One guy was even singing a song about peanuts. There were so many smells in the air, they almost became one. I glanced over at the other three guys, and their faces held the same look as mine must have, a mixture of feeling of everything being awesome and totally out of our league. We stood quietly behind the Green Monster as the world sped by and looked wide-eyed at the big nylon screen hanging so low above the street I felt I could jump up and touch it. I really had nothing to say. It was as if Christmas morning had finally arrived and all you could do was blankly stare at all the wonderful presents that you always wanted in your whole life right there in front of you.

You wanted to ride the new bike, shoot the new BB gun, bounce and throw the new basketball and football, play with the awesome Lionel train set . . . all at the same time!

A vendor behind a huge pushcart selling the "world's best sausages" (it said right above his head) broke my paralysis.

"We goin' in or what?" I said it but couldn't believe it came from me. I should've left the packages wrapped and just imagined what was inside.

"Of course we're goin' in . . . didn't come this far to wimp out." Capisce pounded his glove like a tough guy.

"We are?" Lights looked at me with doubt. "This is kinda rapid here."

Paulie looked at me like a mirror of his twin, except his voice echoed Capisce's. "Yeah, of course, remember? In and out like bank robbers. So, what's the plan, Tags?"

Yeah, what's the plan, Tags? Oh, boy. I glanced down the street, away from their stares and could only think of my father's story. "Let's take a walk. This way." We walked two-by-two down the street, through the crowds of people and slow-moving cars. I didn't think the manhole caper really could work, it was actually pretty dumb, but sometimes you do stupid things and look like a genius later. A little kid in front of me was staring at a lump of ice cream melting on the street and crying his eyes out. He held the empty cone in his hand like a knife. His dad was pleading with him to stop crying. And I thought we had troubles tonight! I watched the ice cream melting all over the street and down into a hole in a manhole cover underneath a parked car. It hit me just then how we were going to sneak into the ballpark.

SIX

"Stop swinging your leg and find the ladder rung, ya big ox!"

"Uh-oh, you're gonna pay for that one, Tags."

Lights smiled at me with a thank-God-it-wasn't-me-that-said-that smile. He was right, Capisce was probably going to give me a knuckle pinch, which was the worst, like getting a zillion plus two bee stings. We called it the helicopter.

"Remind me to helicopter you when I get up there, Tags." Capisce managed to flash a crazed grin as he struggled through the drain hole.

My backside, I thought. "Yeah, sure thing." If you can catch me, dopey. "C'mon. Now get down here before the cops come."

"Knockout!"

Lights' back was to us when we finished pulling Capisce though the drain. His neck was strained looking up and he kept repeating "knockout" except he used a few words that his mother would definitely have fainted cold over hearing. We followed his gaze, and I'm not sure which one of us was the first to realize where we stood, but one by one, our eyes and mouths opened wide and stayed wide. Capisce tossed his arm around me and I steadied myself for the nasty helicopter landing. Instead, he gently put me in a headlock.

"You did it! My man, Tags, you are the bowl of cherries." He gave me a halfhearted noogie and patted me on the back. "Did I ever doubt you? Huh, did I? No, no, no, my superhero. But you did, Lights."

"No way, did not."

Paulie snapped his brother's ear. "Yessir, I heard you."

"You heard squat-olah. I always knew we'd get in."

"Guys, who cares, we're in . . . look." I pointed past their arguing faces and looked up.

We were in if you could believe it. I wasn't sure if I believed it, actually in Fenway Park! In, and without paying! Well, under Fenway Park.

We stood in shocked silence, staring at what I imagined was the foundation of the back of the left-field wall. The four of us were so stone still I began to wonder if anyone was breathing. I nudged Capisce. "Hey, Capisce," I said jokingly, "give me a helicopter just to see if I'm alive."

My dad's story of the guy sneaking into the button factory had seemed like a worthy try, ridiculous but worthy. I had to save face with the guys somehow, or I would be like the guy who strikes out in the bottom of the ninth with the bases chucked; hard to trust next time the game was on the line. Anyway, any idea was better than none.

So while sort of noticing the kid's ice cream melting and dripping down the drain in the manhole cover, my main concern had been to talk the guys into following my brainy plan. We had stopped and bought one "world's best sausage" and split it four ways, Capisce of course grabbing the biggest piece of the pie. As I was enjoying my bite (I don't know about the world's best, but it sure was tasty) I spotted our "in." Beneath a parked car was the manhole cover, our door to the kingdom.

"Capisce, Paulie, Lights . . . listen to me. See that manhole cover over there, under the car? This is what we're gonna do."

With a lot, and I mean a lot of complaining back and forth, we were one, we were The Four Musketeers. I rolled the tennis ball under the parked car as a diversion in case someone was watching and wondering why a kid was underneath a parked car, and Capisce slid beneath first as me and the twins and I cooly leaned against the car's side. Once Capisce had the cover off, he grabbed my ankle and I slid under the cover and down the hole. We had agreed I'd go first.

"Hold my glove. And Capisce? If I don't come back, it's yours." It was the best dead man walking I could muster. If I thought we could get in this way, they'd follow. If I thought we had no chance . . . well, put it this way, they were still going to follow.

My foot found a ladder directly below the opening and I started down. Six big rungs later, my sneaker hit wet concrete. I stood rock still, my heart pounding over the trickle of water under my feet. When I opened my eyes, I was surprised to find a corridor lined with lights. I'd heard about them, and even saw a picture of the corridor once, but never imagined . . . I smiled and squinted. Boy, the lights were very bright. The corridor disappeared around a bend in both directions and was freshly painted in light green and yellow.

Two trolley rails, like the kind in amusement park rides, followed the corridor. I'd heard about this ride years ago from my dad. Right after the strike of 2007, the End-all Strike, as it was known, most thought baseball fans would never go back, tired of the money-hungry baseball players after one year. All I can say is "most" were wrong, and "thank you, baseball gods" for settling whatever the difference was. Well, the Red Sox club would take fans on tours of the ballpark. The old trolley tracks looked like a ride at one of those amusement parks, and the old Fenway was a cathedral of amusement parks; it was the grand old lady, the oldest.

The ground was raised like a pitcher's mound and dry as a bone away from the manhole opening. As I stepped away and into the corridor, I stared in disbelief at a framed picture staring back at me from the concrete wall. It was a Red Sox player from the 1970s. I knew Carlton "Pudge" Fisk like I knew myself. I mouthed Pudge's stats by heart as my body shook with excitement. There in front of me was The Picture! You know, of him waving the ball fair? Over his jersey he had signed it, "To All The Great Fans of Boston, Pudge Fisk." He might as well have signed it to Tags Taglia. The man was a god around my house. It would've been like getting an autograph by God himself and signed to me. Something like, Hang in There, or, Be Good, signed GOD. I ran my fingers over the glass cover and felt a surge of energy. Toss me a ball now, and I'd crush one over the wall to Kenmore Square. My eyes moved at other framed pictures of past stars blanketing the walls. Next to Fisk was Dewey Evans, Luis Tiant, Rico Petrocelli, Carl Yastrzemski, Manny Ramirez, Curt Schilling.

Farther along the corridor were Roger Clemens, Pedro Martinez, then, Joe Cronin, Johnny Pesky, Tris Speaker . . . then Babe Ruth. His Red Sox uniform hung off him like one of Mrs. Beacon's sheets on the clothesline in her backyard. A baby-faced Babe was in full windup delivery, about to let loose a two-seam fastball (what else?). On the bottom of the picture was a scribbled note that I had to laugh at. It read: "To all Sox Fans, Only One of Many to Come!" and signed, "Babe Ruth, 1918." Part of me wanted to cry . . . no, most of me. The other part wanted to laugh so hard I probably would've started crying. I touched Babe's picture, but there was no energy rush like from Pudge's, only sorrow. Maybe the eighty-six years between 1918 and 2004 had absorbed the electrical impulses, or maybe Babe took some of them when the Sox won in '04, sort of like a ghost loosening his grip when the use had diminished. I knew we were going to get those sparks popping again this year. But it would take a really good plan.

Capisce's echoing voice brought me back to the present. (Oh, to be in those stands above me when the Sox finally did win it all again!) I ran back past the wall of stars to the ladder and whispered as loud as I could up to Capisce, "Come on down . . . and bring my glove."

Dead man was still walking, I thought proudly. "Hurry. You're not gonna believe it. It's totally knockout!"

I could hear Capisce giving orders for the other not to screw up and for the last guy to put the cover on, but only half tight so, "we won't stuffacate," or something like that. I waited anxiously by the wall. One by one they stood in front of the wall of the Red Sox with mouths wide open. As a group, I don't believe I ever heard them this quiet.

Now that I think of it, maybe we were this hushed the time when the cop, Skunk Tillman, chased us down the railroad tracks and into Mrs. Fredo's backyard. I had taped two half-dollars (a waste of money, but the half-dollar had the weight and went the farthest) to the train track rail. We waited like bank robbers in the brush for the 3:15 to Boston to speed past. The train would always press the coin so flat and smooth you couldn't tell the pressed mass had been two coins. The train wheels would form them into a perfect "skipping" rock, the kind that could dance over the waves as if God held puppet strings to it.

Lights had double-dared me to hit the crossing guard's old battered tin shack that hadn't been used for a hundred years, maybe more. It was forever a target for all the kids in town. It was so dented and rusty from kids throwing rocks and things at it that it should've been ripped down years ago. Even Spookey Shaw, the town drunk, tried to run it down one night on his way home from another bender, but even then it just dented but didn't die.

I wouldn't have balked at all at the toss (L.C. wouldn't have) except for the fact the shack was one hundred feet away from us . . . and across the intersection of the town square. With the guys egging me on, I couldn't back down, or it would've been, no stopping, go directly to Wimpville for me. So I wound up and let loose (praying I wouldn't knock someone's eye out) with one that surprised even me. The flat coin took off like a missile to Venus. It bounced once off the railroad embankment, ricocheted off Mrs. O'Leary's maple tree, bounced again off the railroad embankment, then flew toward the shack. The coin would've bulls-eyed the old tin warrior right between the eyes if it wasn't for the police car's window . . . well, both windows. The coin had gathered so much speed (I swear to this day it picked up more speed after bouncing off the tree) that it cut through both back windows (no, they're not bulletproof like Capisce thought) and still nicked the top of the tin shack. We all heard the ping of the shack from where we stood, and way before we heard the cop car's siren.

Skunk Tillman took maybe five seconds to realize what had just happened and for him to wheel his car around and drive directly at us . . . on the railroad tracks. With Lights wailing and the four of us trying hard not to pee our pants in fright, we bolted up and over the fence and into Mrs. Fredo's backyard. There we huddled like frightened cats (alley cats, though, tough ones) in the bulkhead of the old lady's cellar for two hours, not talking or breathing, until we all had to go to the bathroom.

≡

"This . . . is . . . the . . . most . . . incredible . . . awesomest . . . knockoutedness . . ."

"Definitely capital Knockout-A-Rooney."

"Tags? Are we where I think we are?"

The three of them stared at the wall, not wanting to blink for fear it would all vanish into a dream. I pointed to the ceiling right above our heads. "Figuring where we came in, the center-field bleachers have to be above us."

"Then . . . we did it! We're in!" Capisce didn't know what to do. I knew he wanted to jump up and down like a mad bear, but instead he bit the leather on his glove to keep from wahooing. "You da man, Tags. Now what?"

The twins high-fived each other and headed for the plaques.

"Paulie, Lights . . . follow me. We gotta keep moving until we're actually in the ballpark. We can come back another time to check out everything."

"Yeah, rapid. Look . . . Yaz, man, and it's signed!"

"They all are, ya peanut brain." Paulie grabbed the corner of Lights' jersey and pulled him to where Capisce and I were heading.

"I knew that," Lights said.

"Guys, keep it down. If we get caught, we're probably grounded for the summer."

Who was I kidding? We'd be grounded for life, or maybe longer. I walked along the trolley line and could hear the faint noise of thirty thousand fans coming in and settling down—the low hum of a powerful motor revving up to full throttle. I peeked over my shoulder to make sure the guys were still with me and I wasn't alone. I wished I was up above, yelling along with the thirty thousand-plus lunatics, but this was kinda rapid, too. In a way I was the heart beating in every one of their bodies. I was in the center of their passions instead of just another drowned-out voice.

The guys were following me, and I felt a little special, powerful, until a door built into the rounded wall opened three feet from me. The lighting wasn't as bright as around the corner from where we had come, which I figured now was center field. I flattened myself against the cool concrete wall like in every army movie I've ever seen, and waved my boys to do the same. Not one of them was paying attention. Capisce must have noticed the lights had dimmed and now was within a hand from me. Paulie and Lights had gotten too close to Capisce and bumped into him, then bumped into me.

This normally would've started a name-calling marathon, but I waved, pushed my shoulders against the wall and quickly made a thumb-over-my-shoulder gesture.

For the first time in our whole history together, they all understood without explanation and pressed themselves against the wall. None of us breathed. The door stood open, but no one exited. The National Anthem played above us as a drip of water echoed from somewhere in the tunnel. I felt a lot like the rats in the tunnel that ran under Concord Avenue from Belmont High School to the Underwood pool.

As bets for soda or candy, we'd walk the pitch-dark quarter-mile tunnel, knowing the whole time that the sounds of scurrying feet all around were those of Ratso's. We never doubted Ratso Risoli lived in the tunnel. If you were able to hear over the beating of your frightened heart, you could hear his howls and cries from the deepest part of the tunnel, even though some old people said it was the wind.

A kid who made the walk (and lived to talk about it) came out feeling like man who survived a war. The walk had to be done, you had to stare down the legend of Ratso or else you'd never be able to look at your friends in the same manner. Ratso's real name was Nicky Risoli, a veteran from the China War of 2009, who rumor had it, lost his face and his arms when a nuclear bomb hit his plane over the South China Sea.

Us guys knew Ratso lived in the tunnel, but what could he do to you? He couldn't see you, and he couldn't grab you, but he supposedly had ears the size of basketball hoops, on account of the nuclear stuff, so he could hear you coming a mile away. The old timers who played checkers in front of the fire station (the ones who didn't say that the howls in the tunnel came from the wind) said that because of his army training, if he caught you, he could chop you in half with his legs, like a scissors kick, and if he really liked you, would eat out your complete insides by burrowing in like a rat after he chopped you in half. I remember crying myself to sleep in fear a few nights after hearing that, but that was when I was a kid.

We grew up hearing about a boy, Percy Hill, who lived the next town over, who was found cut in half and lying next to the train tracks barely fifty feet from the tunnel opening. The cops' story was that he probably committed suicide by lying on the tracks. But we all knew better; if a train hit you, wouldn't you be splatted all over the place, not perfectly sliced in half like how they found Poor Percy Hill. If you asked me and the guys, Ratso's footprints were all over the kid. Some said Poor Percy never left a drop of blood anywhere, which means he didn't have any guts to spill. If you believe the old timers, Ratso must've really liked Poor Percy Hill. So none of us actually walked in the tunnel; although we wouldn't admit it, we all ran like crazies the whole quarter-mile. I ran it once in under three minutes. I swear we all did, even Capisce.

The National Anthem ended and the old stadium rocked above us. Still no one came out of the open door to the room. I was about to wave the guys to go back when a fat man in an electric wheel-chair came shooting out of the door in the wall. He had a laptop computer attached around his waist and a headset worn over a Red Sox cap. He didn't close the door behind him.

I squashed myself against the wall and closed my eyes, waiting for the fat man's shriek of outrage when he saw us standing in a place I knew we weren't supposed to be. Instead, I heard the swish of his rubber tires over the moist cement floor moving away from us. The sound faded slowly, then disappeared. The guys slowly peeled themselves away from the wall and waited for their brave captain (ha!) to give them their orders. All that came to mind was Ratso Risoli waiting with his huge ears against the cool wall, just waiting to cut us in half.

"Tags? What should we do?"

Capisce's whisper made the Ratso image slowly dissolve. I knew he was waiting in the shadows somewhere for someone, but not here and not for us, at least not today.

"We look, what else?"

We kept close to the wall, keeping an ear out for the sound of rubber tires or a voice.

"Keep your eyes and ears open," I whispered to Capisce, "I'll take a peek."

I took a quick glance over the shoulders of the twins for any lurking shadows coming from behind and gave them the thumbs up. I could hear the muffled sound of the fans' voices above as I poked my head in the open doorway. The first thing I was aware of was that the room was empty (no Ratso Risoli today). The second thing was the size of the room; it was tiny, maybe seven feet by six feet, just big enough for the fat guy in the wheelchair to spin around and get out. It also smelled of sweat and cigar smoke, two bad smells made worse when combined. I pinched my nose and stood out of the shadow of the doorway and stared into the room, my mouth dropped open like the fighter plane's bomber doors in the old movies. One by one, the guys sidled up to me to get a look at what we all thought but couldn't voice, "definitely knockout."

"Tags, is that what I think it is?"

"Man, it's right there. You believe this, Lights? Look at it."

"Are you sure that's it?"

"What else could it be? Right, Tags? Is that it?"

It had to be, I thought. What else could it possibly be? We had found "It." Imagine that — the Four Musketeers had stumbled across the "centerpiece of what modern baseball has become," as my father put it. He said everything that stinks in baseball today began when the computer took over. I loved my dad a lot, but it didn't come as a surprise that a guy who sells buttons for a living would hate modern technology.

"That's the thing my dad said ruined baseball. Isn't it, Tags?"

All I could manage was a half-hearted nod as my brain registered the banks of more than a dozen flashing computer screens and more than two dozen rows of knobs and levers; the room had a look of a recording studio.

"It's the Brain." Capisce nudged past me and stood in the middle of the tiny room. He looked like a bear in his den. "We found the Brain, guys. We actually found the freakin' Brain."

"What's the thing do?"

Paulie looked at his brother as if he had just asked the dumbest question in the history of the world.

"The Brain, Lights. It's, you know, the Brain," Paulie whispered impatiently to his twin.

"Oh, you mean . . ."

"Yeah, exactly. Whatta you think I meant?"

We all nodded like bobblehead dolls in a wind storm. It was the Brain, the control center of all the balls and strikes, safes and outs.

"So," Paulie chimed quietly, "tell Lights what it does, Tags."

So I did, repeating what my dad told me. There was only one umpire in baseball now. The rest were shown the door five years ago, and I'm sure nobody cried. Now all pitches were called by an electronic field by sensors placed in the baseballs. The batter's box was electronically squared, a perfect box from the hitter's letters across his chest to his knees, made by a centerfield camera. When the pitch came through to the catcher, the sensor in the baseball would register to the preset computerized strike zone whether the pitch was a ball or strike. If the ball was hit foul, the computer could register where and if the ball broke the electronic plane surrounding the field. Even the base paths and bases had sensors. The base paths were lined with sensors to read fair or foul balls. Sensors were placed in the players' shoes. They were checked every at bat by a special sensor-testing mat in the batter's box. The idea was to catch ballplayers' tampering with them, to register if they stayed inside the base paths. The bases had sensors that could read if the foot reached the base before the ball hit the glove.

The only nonplayer on the field was one umpire who stood behind the pitcher and called outs, like fly-ball outs. On a close play at a base, a manager could challenge the umpire's call but he would be chancing an extra strike or a ball to be added to the hitter's count. A computerized printout to the tenth of a second from the moment the ball reached the base and when the foot hit the bag could be displayed on the center-field screen, but only after the play.

Each manager had two challenges during nine innings. The umpire would review the play if the manager thought the computer or umpire were blind (my dad never thought the computer was right). If the manager was wrong in his argument, either a strike or a ball would be added to the count to the next batter. After a year in use, managers' complaints were way down.

On the top of the fences were sensors to determine if the ball cleared the wall. Almost every part of the game was now done by a computer and electronics. Human error had been removed and replaced by software and the Brain. Every ballpark had a Brain, and every park had a guy that programmed it, I suppose like the fat guy in the wheelchair.

In the five years of using the Brain, the chance of a game being decided by an umpire's mistake had all but disappeared; it was the

Oz of baseball, and the thing that ruined baseball. Our fathers hated it because perfection is easier to hate than imperfection. I guess I never really thought about it one way or another. You grow up with something, you take it for granted without much thought.

But now, staring at the "centerpiece of baseball," I felt like I just kissed my first girl. At least I thought that's what it must feel like—new, different, and very knockout.

At the end of the tiny room, a device that looked like a camera was placed on top of a tripod that stood on a table. The device had a long lens, telescopic, I guessed, that was pressed up against a small plastic window. Wires and chords wandered in and out of the camera thing and lay on the floor in a tangled bunch. I figured the device was the eye for the Brain. One at a time, we took a peek out the plastic window, careful not to touch the lens.

Fenway Park, green as a summer leaf, stood right before us like a beautiful monument. Directly in front and slightly below us, Sox centerfielder Marquis Dupree, number 40, played catch with left-fielder Jellybean Otto. They were warming up before the game and I was maybe three feet from Dupree! I bit my tongue to keep from screaming out how downright knockout this whole scene was. Capisce began pulling at me to get a look. I tried to ignore him until he almost pulled my arm off.

"Be careful of the wires. We don't want to upset anything," I warned him.

"Yeah, yeah, I know. What's out there?"

Capisce stepped in front of me and I nearly backed into the tripod. I already had it all figured out. The camera took an instant picture of the pitch in a predetermined strike zone according to the height of the batter, from his jersey letters to his knees. The information was then sent to the computer which recorded it. A robotic voice, like the voice in an elevator, then boomed out over the PA system whether it was a strike or ball. Which meant the camera was placed exactly where it would record the pitches. Which also meant if the camera was moved, it would throw the whole strike zone out of whack.

I smiled like a slick cat. The Plan was starting to take form.

Capisce was just about to turn to me and say something when the camera started to rotate left. It nearly knocked him in the head.

The camera buzzed to a stop and quickly rotated right, up, then down. It repeated the motion and then settled directly to center.

"What'd you do? You touch anything?"

Paulie jumped back from the camera and almost fell over Capisce.

"Nah, nuthin' . . . I swear."

"It follows the path of the ball," I said quietly. I wasn't sure at first but it started making more sense now. Of course. The sensors in the ball were picked up by the sensors in the camera and relayed to the computers. It was just going through the pregame maneuvers to test the system.

"What does?" Capisce made sure he stepped carefully over the bundle of wires strewn over the floor.

"The camera's actually the eye for the computer. It's probably the real brain because it's the thing the computer needs to call the strikes, balls and outs. If that's moved, or worse, busted, the computer doesn't know what's going on." It was a guess but I figured an accurate one.

"Tags, I say we get out of here. We get caught in here, we're fried dough." Lights backed out of the room and glanced in the direction the chair guy headed.

"C'mon Lights, don't be such a wuss. Whatta you think would happen if I flip the camera upside down?"

Paulie pretended to reach for the camera. "Like this."

"Don't do nuthin', Paulie! Tags, tell him not to touch nuthin'."

"He's not gonna touch anything, Lights." I couldn't agree more, though this wasn't the time.

"Lights is right, guys," I said to the others. "Not now. We know more than we need. Especially where everything is." I really did want to look around a little bit longer. "We'll come back when the Sox leave town, it'll give us some peace time."

Lights repeated my thought. "Yeah, peace time . . . good thinking."

"We're in, though, might as well sneak into the game." Capisce looked at me as if to say what else is there to do?

"Might as well." We all agreed.

The four of us walked out slowly and carefully followed the path the wheelchair guy took. It zigzagged down a corridor maybe ten feet wide for about ten minutes, past the Red Sox players' pictures.

We stood dazed as the corridor ended at a brick wall. How could the path just end?

"Are you sure that guy came this way?"

"What's the matter with you, Lights? We were standing against the wall watching him go here, remember?" Paulie's voice was a little unsure.

"What I meant is that maybe he took . . ."

It was then I noticed the elevator behind Capisce. "There. That's where he went."

The guys followed my gaze. Built into the wall was an elevator door that looked just wide enough for one wheelchair. There was one button on the side of the door, UP.

"Guys, we can't take that elevator." I looked at the three of them with pleading eyes.

"Why not, Tags? We can't turn back now."

"I'm not saying we can't go, Capisce. I'm thinking only one of us should go. More of a chance of getting away if someone nabs us."

"How we gonna decide who goes? The usual?"

"Count me out. I'll stay put." Lights was looking back down the winding path.

"Okay. Lights, you flip. The one who doesn't match the other two goes. Agreed?"

Lights took my quarter and flipped. Heads for Paulie, heads for Capisce, tails for me. It came up tails.

"Oh man, I wanted to go," Paulie said. "Maybe two of us should go, kinda watch out for the other guy."

"Maybe next time, Paulie. Okay. This is the deal. Wait for me at the bottom of the steps. I'll come back if there's a clean, safe way in. If you hear me yelling, bolt fast. Here, take my glove, Capisce."

"What if you get caught?" Capisce took the glove out of my hand with a quick swipe. "They'll probably arrest you and throw you into jail."

"Nice goin', Capisce, we hadn't thought of that." Lights said.

"All right. Wait ten minutes for me. If I'm not at the ladder by then, you guys go and we'll meet at the path to the tracks."

"Ten minutes? Lights, what time's L.C. saying?" Paulie had to hang on to his brother to keep him from walking back down the corridor without them. It was seven-ten. "I'll see you in ten minutes."

"Yeah, but Tags...what if when we get to the tracks and you still aren't back, what then?"

Yeah, what then, I thought. I'll probably have been caught, arrested, jailed, and worse, my parents would have had to come to the cop station and bail me out. Might as well say goodbye to me until I'm eighteen because grounded for life looked like a given.

"Wait 'til eight o'clock, then head back to the tent. I'll catch up to you one way or another. And Capisce, watch the glove."

"Aye-aye, mon cap-i-tano." Capisce mock saluted me. "All right, you grunts, you heard the commander, to the ladder. Let's go, march it straight."

I stood alone in the cool cellar air of Fenway Park and watched the guys march out of sight. With the quiet around me, the noise from above—the fans, the vendors, and the music—seemed amplified. In a way I felt very knockout, grown-up in a daring way. On the other hand, my own stupid thoughts of getting caught sat heavy on my shoulders.

The elevator button (Dad would've liked that) lit white under my finger. I imagined the entire Boston police squad pouring out of the tiny elevator and arresting me. Instead, the door opened quietly and politely waited for my decision.

Should I risk the rest of my summer and possibly my life? Or should I just skip it and make up a killer story of how I escaped twenty gun-waving Boston cops like a hero?

I stepped into the elevator. The doors closed, and there I was, trapped inside the belly of a submarine at the bottom of the Atlantic. I held my breath, but it was so quiet that I could hear the blood pounding in my ear drums. I swallowed hard to stop the beating and noticed the one button with a simple UP arrow on the wall in front of me.

One floor? If there was security, I'd have to be quick. My hand shook a little as the arrow lit red, the color of trouble under my finger. The submarine was now rising off the bottom of the deep.

The elevator stopped.

I held my breath and stood to the side of the opening door. Crowd noises replaced the pounding of my heart. I could hear the thick Boston calls of "Hey, beer!" and "Popcorn here!" not far from where I stood. I was in. Half of me was ready to explode in excitement, the other in fright. I steadied my legs and couldn't imagine what my friends were going to say when I told them I'd actually made it into the park. I'd be a hero for at least a day. I stepped out of the elevator. A wall of people walked two feet in front of me going in every direction. Cups of beer and soda were splashing all over their shoes and on the kids unlucky enough to be the wrong height, while other fans holding children and popcorn and sponge fingers and pennants, bumped into each other like the fiercest bumper-car rink I ever saw. They all went about their business like robots with sticky soles, a little slow but moving anyway. I didn't want to join them, but at the same time, I didn't want to be apart. Except, I never got the chance. Did you ever get a feeling something is about to happen before it actually does? Like two or three seconds before a ballplayer hits one out and you just know it's coming?

I was about to blend in when I heard the voice meant for me. It was low at first, but somehow louder than the crowd.

"Hey, you!"

I turned back to the elevator.

"I'm talkin' to you, kid!"

The doors to the elevator had closed. My days of freedom were over; bring on the rock pile, boss man, I'm ready to break them rocks. I looked for the guy behind the voice as my hand felt for the elevator button.

"You . . . kid, were you in that elevator? Whatta you doin' near that elevator?"

He was a big guy, and I mean big, probably weighed three hundred pounds, and carried a club that looked like Capisce's baseball bat. He was twenty feet from me and moving fast, as fast as a three-hundred guy could, I guessed. My hand pressed the button . . . c'mon, c'mon. He was having a hard time getting through the crowd of people because of his size. For a split-second I could swear he eyed the hot dog vendor on the way by. I could see the sweat pouring off his forehead and his stomach pulling up to his chins as he tried to suck in air. Not only will they arrest me for sneaking into Fenway, I thought, they're going to get me for murder if this guy drops dead. I took my eyes off him for a second and then realized why the elevator hadn't returned. I'd been pushing a key hole, there was no button . . . there was no way out!

He reached out to me with the sweatiest, meatiest hand I ever saw. I think I shrieked, but that I wouldn't tell my friends. My legs decided to separate themselves from my brain just as his hand touched my shoulder. I turned and ran straight into a man holding two cups of beer. He shouted at me, but I'd already raced by him and started running down a ramp. Faces and objects were blurs as I darted out of the ramp and into what seemed like a million fans walking around like zombies from a horror movie. If it was a movie, it could be named The Snack Bar Zombies, or, Return of the Snack Bar People. In any case, no one would've cared if I was the Slasher of Fenway Park as long as they got their beer. I slowed down, looked over my shoulder and finally reached a walk. I backtracked from where I guessed I had come in and went to the end of the concrete walkway. One more quick look over my shoulder. Section number 33 glared at me from the top of the ramp.

At the top, I finally saw it—Fenway Park, the Green Monster— so much more beautiful in reality than I ever envisioned. The monster went as high as the sky, the net reaching for the heavens. If heaven had a baseball park, it would be just like this. For the first time in my life, I stood in the company of greatness, of beauty, of . . .

"Kid . . . stay . . . right . . . there."

The heavyweight's white shirt was soaked through and he couldn't put two words together without gasping and wheezing. I had to hand it to him for not giving up, though. He barreled up the ramp like an avalanche going backward. I took a mental snapshot of the park and realized my welcome was over. I took off toward home plate, ran down another ramp and raced for the exit door. Once through the gate, I turned toward the railroad tracks, my heart racing a zillion miles an hour. I couldn't believe what I'd just done. I wanted to scream, just go crazy. I'd made it, plus escaped from the cops! Wait 'til the guys hear this!

The evening sky was darkening and the traffic had slowed. A few late-arriving fans wandered outside the red-numbered gates. I overheard a couple of guys scalping tickets. I felt like turning around and yelling "Not me, baby!" I cut between the parking lot and the warehouses and could see my friends walking up the path toward the tracks. My head buzzed with excitement as I sprinted the final hundred yards.

That night we didn't sleep as I told them my story. I know I didn't sleep the next night either . . . or the next. In fact, the four of us didn't sleep for the rest of the summer as the Plan was beginning to seem ever more necessary.

The beginning of September was here, with only three days left before school started. The Red Sox had lost the ten-game lead in the division. With only a month to go, they led the Yankees by three games. L.C. was having another L.C. year; three twenty-two batting average, twenty-six home runs, ninety-two runs batted in, but the rest of the team had taken the usual early vacation.

The town was in a frenzy. You couldn't read a sports page without gloom about where the Sox were heading. Management was trying to paint a pretty picture, but after twenty years of failure, and moving agonizingly slowly into another eighty-six years, they would've had to hire every single one of the great Italian Renaissance painters to get the fans to believe. Series tickets were rumored to have been printed (some guy who bought buttons from my dad said he had heard that because he sold buttons to the Red Sox for their jerseys) which added to our paranoia. The players were saying all the right things, but we were afraid we knew better.

The four of us were trying to enjoy the last full days of summer, and we didn't need the Red Sox to fall flat on their faces. But just in case, the Plan was close to final.

"Tags, when the cop pulled the gun on you…did you really say, 'Not today, copper?'"

"Lights, how many times you gonna ask him that? For cryin' out loud." Paulie was lying on his back, but he still managed to boot his brother in the behind.

Twotails rolled in the dirt and grass next to my head. Today was a hot one, ninety-five degrees. We had decided to take an early lunch break, the heat and the Red Sox weighing a little heavier on us today than usual. I stared at Twotails. Even with a handful of sticky burrs hanging off her bum, which normally would set me off in a laughing fit, I could manage just a tiny chuckle. Twotails rolled and blinked at me as if to ask if she had to do everything around this place. The guys depended on me.

I stood, hiked up my pants and shrugged my shoulders like a tough guy I'd seen on television. I wiped my nose and talked nasally like a thug. "Not tuhday, coppah! Oh no, not tuhday."

I ran toward first base, darted to second, cut sharply toward third, and slid into home, sending up a storm of brown dust. The guys stood and cheered, greeting me with high-fives and slapping and punching each other in better spirits. Twotails licked her paws in order to get the dirt to stick better and then looked at me like it had been her idea. The whole scene had taken a couple of minutes, but as soon as we had laughed and yelled, the guys went back to silent sprawling on the infield. This was as bad as I had seen them.

"Hey, Lights, what time does L.C. say it is?" I hoped it was near twelve, this was getting depressing.

"Eleven-oh-eight." Lights' voice was low and dull.

"Who wants to go over the Plan?" I have to try something, I thought desperately.

Capisce sat up first. "Yeah, yeah, yeah. Let's go over the Plan."

"Yeah, you never can be too sure, you know, just in case we need to use it." Paulie joined Capisce's enthusiasm.

"Gotta be sure we got everything just right. Right, Tags?" Lights patted Twotails excitedly.

So we went over the Plan again, for the hundred-zillion-millionth time . . . just in case.

"I say we have a run-through. We go back to school the day after tomorrow. We can tell our parents we're having a sleep-out over at your house, Lights and Paulie, you know, for the last one of the summer, then head into the game. We try our Plan, but not really."

$$=$$

The sun was setting on another scorcher of a day. The four of us were lounging after dinner like fat cats on the back steps of the Beacons' house. Twotails was busy chasing a moth around the backyard or she would've been lounging with us. The clinking of dinner plates echoed through opened windows, a noise I loved. It meant family and togetherness, the summer and my friends . . . and baseball, especially baseball. Open windows meant warm weather, which meant spring, which meant spring training, which meant baseball season, which meant summer.

Departing and approaching seasons gave us hope, but as this one exited we were getting concerned. A cicada buzzed a symphony from somewhere in the yard as the summer night began its slow advance.

"Whatta you mean, 'not really try' our Plan, Tags?" Capisce frowned at me.

Twotails darted into the bushes and got stuck. "Just like it sounds. We sneak in like we did before and everyone does their job like we've talked about and gone over and over for the past month. Except, we don't do anything. It's called a dry run, to see if we really can pull it off."

"Why not give it a shot? We're gonna be taking a chance sneaking in, why not go for the whole ball of snow?"

Paulie broke into a laugh. "That's wax, Capisce. Ball of wax." Paulie looked at Capisce and realized he probably shouldn't have corrected him. "But snow's rapid, means the same. Doesn't it, Tags?"

Twotails bolted out of the bushes and did a somersault, landing on her belly with a thud. She looked around stunned, then dropped her head onto her paws, most likely exhausted from all the tussling. Her eyes slowly closed shut; I felt like doing the same.

"One of these days I'm gonna pop you like a couple of rotten grapes." Capisce never looked at either of the brothers.

This kind of teasing went on all the time. No one meant anything by what they said, which we all knew, but each of us knew exactly how to get under the others' skin. Paulie teased Capisce because he knew he could outrun him. Capisce teased Lights because Lights wasn't quick enough to get a return zinger in that made any sense. Paulie and Lights teased each other because, well, because they were brothers. The only one who didn't get teased was me. They'd give me a mouthful of hard time, but rarely did they tease me. I'm not sure why that was.

Maybe they looked to me as the wise one, the one with the answers to the burning questions that twelve-year-olds have, like, What exactly is that thing in the center of a baseball? Or what exactly is Goofy from the old Walt Disneys? Is he a dog?

"We can't pull it off yet. If something goes wrong now, we won't be able to pull the job off when we really need to. Plus, there's no need right now—the Sox are still in first place."

"Yeah, but the lead's goin' in the toilet, and fast," Paulie said. "It's only three games, Tags. Maybe Capisce is right, maybe this is the time."

"No, no, no. It's like in the war, guys, you wait 'til you see the whites of their eyes. If we shoot early and miss, and the Red Sox need us come crunch time, and we're not there . . . what then? We got to hold off as long as we can, be patient, you know? We have to stick to our Plan, no matter what."

"What if we're too patient? You ever think of that?"

"Capisce, I've thought of everything. You have to trust me. Lights, the time please?"

It was starting to get dark earlier, which was just another reminder of the closing of the season. I didn't like it, but I didn't fret about it either.

"Six-oh-one."

We finally agreed about the trial run and split up to tell our parents about the sleep-out at the Beacons'. We were back and on the road in under ten minutes, with Twotails sitting not so snugly inside the tent in the Beacons' backyard.

"Who's pitching tonight Tags?"

We walked the tracks, gloves in hand, discussing the pitching match-ups and skipping stones. Statistics and arguments about who were the best ball players bounced around like the flat rocks we tossed.

We got off the tracks and melded into the human traffic around the old ballpark. The same fantastic food odors and excitement hit us immediately, but something else hung heavy in the air that wasn't present on our last visit; the fans seemed hesitant. I noticed a difference in their smiles now. Maybe it was just my uneasiness about another Red Sox collapse, my imagination playing itself out on every face in Red Sox Nation. Or quite possibly it did exist in every heart and soul that had crossed this very spot for over the last twenty years. It was anguish hidden beneath hope. I wanted to reach out and grab the father who held his son's hand and tell him quietly, "Don't worry, everything's under control. Tell your son he'll be watching the World Series Champion Boston Red Sox! Tell him we're gonna fix everything."

It would've made me feel better, but Red Sox fans by nature are pessimistic, so they would've just thought I was crazy.

We stood like soldiers across the street from the manhole cover at the tunnel entrance. I looked it over with a safecracker's chilly eye. The rear wheel of a car was sitting a little closer to the manhole cover than I liked, but I didn't think it would cause us any problems. After splitting two "world's best sausages," we were ready. I hesitated but rolled the tennis ball under the car anyway, and Capisce went at it like a champion retriever. Thirty seconds later, I was through the opening and helping Lights down the ladder. After the usual Capisce difficulties, we were all standing in the damp basement of Fenway Park.

"Remember, stay close to the wall. We've got to time this just right. Lights, the time?"

"Six-fifty-six."

"If I'm right, wheelchair guy should be coming out of the room right after the National Anthem. Keep track of the time, Lights."

I wanted to read every plaque and statistic that covered the cellar wall, but instead I played the commander in chief. Touching my lips with my finger to keep the guys quiet, I motioned them to press their bodies against the cool wall.

"Remember, keep very close to the wall . . . and no talking," I whispered.

We inched our way around the bend. Ten feet from where we stood, a dim light shone through a slightly open door of the Brain room. I held what little breath I had and listened for the cue.

"It's seven on the nose, Tags," Lights whispered in my ear.

A faint National Anthem ended. Half a minute later, I heard the sound of rubber wheels on damp cement and the low hum of a motor going in the other direction. I counted to thirty and pushed off the wall; the guys followed suit. We were at the open door without a hitch.

With gloves in hand instead of guns, my soldiers stormed Brain Central.

"Knockout, guys." Capisce punched me on the soldier. "I'm lookin' first this time." Capisce bulled past us with a snort.

The room seemed the same; white computer cable wires zigzagged around the confined room, mounds of them coiled like snakes on the green, cement floor, reminding me of the dirty pile of clothes under my bed. The cigar smell was ever-present. It stunk, but it lent some old-guy toughness to what we were doing. I surveyed the wires and camera. Pulling this off was going to be ice cream.

"C'mon Capisce, let me have a look."

Paulie, then Lights, took turns looking through the plastic window that was the camera's view. It struck me in a funny way how easy this seemed, that quite possibly it wasn't as hard as I first thought. Capisce's words stuck in my mind about taking a shot. Heck, how often are you inside the belly of the beast and don't kick out a little?

"Tags, I think maybe, just maybe now, we can take a tiny gamble. You know, for one pitch?" I looked at Capisce and saw all my planning and scheming being flushed down the toilet whether I liked it or not. The Plan still belonged to me, I owned the rights and called the shots, but big business was muscling in and its name was Capisce.

"Yeah, I was thinking the same." I said the words but they didn't come from me, at least they didn't feel as if they did. "But only for one pitch."

"Geez, Tags, how we gonna know if it works if it's only for one pitch?"

Paulie and Lights heard our whispers and gathered around.

"Oh, believe me, we'll know." The angle of the one pitch had to be so off that I had no doubt the red flag would be thrown and the troops sent in. It had to be done that way. We'd have time to adjust the Plan at another time . . . if we didn't get caught. "If we do it, and the one pitch goes off line, then they'll have to send someone down here to check on it. If that's the case, then we're not gonna have a lot of time to bolt."

"I dunno, Tags, it sounds dangerous. Doesn't it, Paulie? Capisce, I thought we were . . ."

"Zip it, Lights. We're in this together or not at all." Capisce glanced at us and figured what was the best approach. "Ok, we'll flip. Tails we don't, heads we do. Sound fair? Tags?"

"Sounds fair. Paulie? Lights? You guys in?"

"In like an L.C. slide." Paulie whacked his brother's shoulder. "Lights is in too. Ain't ya, Lights?"

"If we get caught, we'll be in the closet for two months." Lights looked at us and realized he sounded a little like a crybaby.

"But that's the chance you gotta take, right? If you guys are in, then I'm in."

"Who's got the coin?" Capisce held out his meaty paw.

As I pulled a quarter out of my jeans, Lights and Paulie argued over who was going to flip.

"I'm flipping, guys." I placed my new glove next to my foot. "Heads we're in, tails we split." I showed them the two sides of the coin like a football referee in case of any unforeseen screw-ups.

The four of us stood in a tight circle, each one glancing at the other for reassurance. I almost scrapped the new Plan but had already released the coin into the air. The flip was one of my personal best, tight and straight, just barely missing the ceiling. The quarter hit on its edge in the dead center of our circle and shot between Capisce's legs and underneath the table that held the camera.

"That's bad luck, guys. You all know we can't use that quarter again."

Lights was right. Our rules stated that you couldn't reflip with the same quarter. And you couldn't flip with anything but a quarter—no penny, no nickel, no dime, no half-dollar, no silver dollar.

"Okay, who's got a quarter?"

"I'm out." Paulie didn't have to look.

"Me too." Lights pulled his pockets inside out and held out his empty palms.

Capisce was halfway under the table that held the camera and tripod and crawling farther under it until all that was sticking out into the room was his size ten pair of dirty-white sneakers.

"Capisce, forget it we can't use that quarter. You know the rules." Lights looked at me, shaking his head.

"I got it." Capisce backed up and began to haul himself up. In a flash of the moment where you see things happening before they do, I started to tell Capisce to be careful . . . but I never got it out. As he proudly got up with the quarter in his hand, his shoulder banged heavily into the corner of a table covered with computers.

In agonizingly slow motion, a computer tilted and fell, taking with it another computer that was attached to it, then another, then another. In a domino effect, they fell on and around a cowering Capisce. We watched them fall. Then I heard Lights gasp for breath.

"Holy . . . the Brain!"

Lights pointed at the camera that called the balls and strikes. The Brain sat firmly on the table Capisce had hit, but its cable wires were attached to the now spilled computers. The Brain teetered on one leg of the tripod, then rocked on the other, then fell. The whole nightmare had taken three seconds, if that. Capisce was wrapped in cable wires, his arms and legs entangled like a marionette.

"We're dead we're screwed we're cooked we're . . ."

"Lights, shut up!" Paulie grabbed his brother's arm and pulled him toward the door.

Capisce had pulled himself out of the wires and away from the computers and almost beat the Beacon twins out the door. Me? I had to hang around for a minute longer to find out if what we thought we were doing was actually what we were doing, if you can understand that logic. I stepped over the fallen computers and bundles of wires and looked through the plastic window that now had nothing in the way of my view. I'm not sure what I was searching for; players pointing toward the square window as my face was plastered against it? Police running onto the field? The scoreboard lights blowing up in a computer meltdown? What was surprising was that nothing happened. There was no chaos or confusion, no police pointing guns at my curious face. I looked at the black number 24 on the back of the Tigers' center-fielder Zak Murray as he played toss with his left fielder.

As I watched the slow toss, it occurred to me why nothing seemed out of place. If the camera in question was the main computer keeping track of the pitches, and I had no doubt it was, then there should've been an immediate response and shutdown of the main frame. The reason why no one had noticed a difference was that the whole episode had happened between innings. But I guessed the people who ran these computers weren't far away. They'd have to know something had happened, which meant they were coming. But I had to see for myself.

"Wallace!" I peered through the plastic window as Hal Wallace strode to the plate. I had faintly heard the crowd chanting, "Wallace! Wallace!" earlier as he loosened up in the batter's box. "C'mon Hal, you can do it, my man, start it off . . . ."

My heart stopped and my eyes felt as if they popped clear out of my head. The one umpire who stood on the field threw his arms in the air and turned on his heels toward me. What I had expected to happen earlier did so as surely as my name is Tags Taglia. Everyone turned and looked . . . directly at me.

"HOLY JUMPIN'. . . IT WORKED!" I screamed and bolted out of the room. It does work! it really does work! it is the Brain, my mind shrieked as I sprinted down the tunnel. Wait 'til the guys hear . . . I stopped dead in my tracks.

Paulie, Lights and Capisce were running toward me. If I hadn't stopped, the collision would've been ugly. As it was, Paulie slammed me pretty hard, sending me toppling backward and nearly over. As Paulie stopped, Lights, then Capisce, banged into each other like cartoon bowling pins. We caught each other, then began yelling.

"It worked!"

"We're dead!"

"We're stuck in here."

"Whatta we do now?"

"You shoulda saw it . . . it works!"

"My parents are gonna kill us . . . our parents . . . "

"We're trapped like rats."

"It really works?"

"Yeah, it does."

"But they're on their way, they saw me."

"What difference does it make when you're dead?"

Then it struck me. "What? Whatta you mean, stuck in here?"

"Capisce thinks the man . . ."

"Hey Paulie, I can answer for myself."

"Whatever. But you're the one who put the cover back." Paulie moved a tiny bit farther away from Capisce.

"Beacon, I swear . . ." Capisce scrunched his face like an angry bull.

"Guys, guys, c'mon, we don't have much time. Tell me what's going on."

Capisce turned his attention from Paulie and looked at me. "The manhole cover won't budge. I've tried putting all my strength into moving it, but it won't move."

"Oh boy, we're fried dough, guys."

"Lights, cool it, will you? We're not cooked, yet." I looked quickly behind me; Lights wasn't too far off the mark.

"I got an idea." We headed around the bend and back toward our exit. "Paulie, keep an eye on our backs." I was really hoping beyond hope that what I was thinking would turn out to be our problem.

"I hear a bell, Tags. Oh no, they're coming. You think it's the elevator?"

I had heard it echo down the tunnel, also. "Sounds like it, Paulie. We just might be fried dough if we don't hurry."

I grabbed the first rung of the ladder and climbed as fast as a monkey. Standing just below the manhole cover, I tried to figure where the tire was that blocked our exit. I hit the corner of the steel cover with the palm of my hand with all my strength; it didn't move. I hit it harder but did nothing but give myself a stinger of the hand; it felt like catching a line drive in the cold. It had to move unless someone else had parked right on top of it. One more time I smacked it and felt my shoulder move but not the cover.

"Capisce, can you get up here?" I glanced below and Capisce was practically in my face before I had finished the sentence. "Hit right here," I pointed to the spot that had to be right.

"Guys, hurry, I hear voices."

Capisce stood on a rung below me. He looked at his hand as if he was warning it not to do him wrong, then spit a pretty good-size ball into his palm for a better grip. With a snort, he hit the corner of the cover with all his strength; it shot up and out like a rocket. But because the car was parked so close, the cover clanged off the bottom of the car with such force it came back at us as if it was on a rubber band. It was then Capisce did something that probably saved our lives. Instead of allowing the metal cover to slam back onto the cement he caught it like a pop up in the soft webbing of his glove.

His glove!

"My glove!" I scared Capisce so much he almost fell off the ladder. "I forgot my glove!"

"No time, Tags! We gotta split."

"No, no, I gotta get the glove!" I started down the ladder but Capisce grabbed me by the shirt collar and pulled. I kicked and flailed my arms, but Capisce's hold was like a bear's. Lights and Paulie were pushing me up as hard as they could.

"My dad's gonna ground me for life," I whined.

"Our dads are gonna ground us all for life if we don't get moving. Forget your glove, Tags."

"No way. That glove was a present from my father." There, I said it, but immediately wished I hadn't.

"That glove, was a present? Hey guys, Tags' father bought him that glove."

"No!" The Beacons were one. "Tags' daddy bought him the glove?" They started to sing:

"Daddy Taglia, Daddy Taglia, buys me a glove . . .

Daddy Taglia, Daddy Taglia, Tags is in love?"

It was a pretty stupid song, but I had to admit, it wasn't all that bad considering they thought it up right there on the spot.

"Isn't that sweet, your daddy bought you a glove?" Capisce let me fall off the ladder and past the twins as I landed with a thud on my butt. They couldn't stop laughing and singing as they bolted through the opening and to freedom.

"Guys, don't leave me here," I pleaded, but it was too late. I looked over my shoulder and down the barrel of a .38 special. The cop leveled it at my eye and spoke in a manner warning every nerve in my frozen body.

"Well, well, punk, we gotcha."

"I didn't do it I didn't do it I didn't do it I didn't do. . . ."

"Tags, shut up, you'll wake my parents." Lights' voice came from behind a beam of light. He was sitting in a corner of the tent with a flashlight in my eyes and telling me to shut up, and I didn't have a clue why.

"What did you have, a bad dream?"

I groped under the pillow of my sleeping bag and found my glove. It was just a bad dream. The whole ordeal was just a stomach-ache of a bad dream. The four of us were sleeping out in the Beacons' backyard. Now I remembered. We had gone to Fenway, but there had been a car parked over the manhole cover, blocking our entrance. After eating a couple of sausages, we scratched the Plan and came home.

"Yeah, a very bad dream." I held the glove tight and vowed it would never leave my sight again.

"How bad?" Capisce was awake too.

"Who had a bad dream?" Paulie asked no one in particular.

"Tags did. Didn't you hear him?"

"No, I was sleeping."

"So what was it?"

They were all sitting up in their sleeping bags staring at me, including Twotails at my feet, waiting for my horror story of a bad dream. So I told them, and added, of course, how I took a hail of bullets for them as they escaped to freedom.

"You all owe me big time." We all had a laugh with a few insults tossed in then went back toward the comfort of sleep. Except for me.

The day of actually following through with our Plan was nearing fast. The radio had given us the bad news; the Red Sox had lost again tonight and the Yankees had won. The lead was now down to two games with twenty-seven remaining. I thought about the gun in my face and scrunched my eyes shut trying to get the vision to disappear. When the time came to pull it off, even with a gun in my face, I was going to be ready. I owed it to the city and to the long-suffering fans.

SEVEN

We met at the Beacons' house after our first day of school and immediately headed over to the Pit. Days were getting shorter as the season slowly turned. If we hurried, the we could squeeze in five innings at the Pit, but that didn't diminish our enthusiasm or shorten our complaints about the Red Sox. They had lost again last night, and the Yankees had won. The lead had been trimmed to one game.

"What'd I tell you guys?" Capisce was beside himself with anger. "Every year it's the same thing."

"Every year? You're starting to sound like our dads." I lay on my back and tossed the ball in the air as straight as I could, but for some unknown reason that is nearly impossible to do; it fell a foot over my head. I retrieved it and tossed it again.

"You know what I mean. You've read all the books. Every year it's something."

"Yeah, but not this year, right, Tags?"

"This year's different, Tags. Tell Capisce."

The Beacon twins always echoed you when they needed to be reassured, and I'd become the resident assurer, apparently.

"Yeah, yeah, yeah, this year's different, your mama." Capisce angrily grabbed his Cobra bat and hammered the ground around home plate. "Read the books—1946, 1975, 1978, 2003! Oh, and in case you guys forgot, how 'bout '86, perhaps? Maybe the walkout in 2022 shakes your memory? We were in first freakin' place, the best team in the league, and they cancel the World Series. You guys remember that? We're doomed in this town. It's always something."

Capisce stopped pounding the ground and lay down as if in defeat. "So what makes you think this year's any different, you boneheads? Different years same results, mark my words."

"Not this year, me buckos." My toss landed five feet from my head and I crawled to retrieve the ball and to try again. "We'll pull this caper off." I was starting to sound tough even to myself. "Don't you worry. I've dreamed the whole thing. In my dream, we sneak into Fenway, pull off the perfect crime and become heroes forever. The only problem is, nobody knows."

"That sucks if nobody knows." Lights said.

"It might, yeah. But it's got to be that way, Lights, or we all go to prison for breaking and entering and anything else the cops decide to charge us with."

My toss went up and hit Capisce in the belly. He flipped it to me without an argument.

"Knowing how difficult it's going to be to keep our mouths shut, we've got to promise each other that we never ever ever ever say a thing about what we're about to do, and when it goes down, nothing about what we did. We've got to promise on that or we can't do it."

"We gotta promise to tell no one? For the rest of our lives?"

"We can't tell for the rest of our lives?"

"Seems stupid to do it and not tell."

"Guys, listen to me." I got off my back and stood in the middle of them. "If I have to tell you one more time, I'm gonna pop. Right here, right in the middle of you guys, I'm gonna explode into tiny little pieces, and all these buttons on my shirt are going to be like missiles and make you all blind. So listen closely!" I talked as slowly as possible without sounding as if I was talking under water.

"What we are doing is illegal, ill-le-gull. Understand? Comprende? Got it? It's against the law, it's cheating, it's stealing, it's all those things and more. We are fixing the outcome of a game, if we can. Which I know we can. And by fixing the outcome, we're committing a crime as bad as, you should know, Capisce, you read the sports history books."

"The 1919 Black Sox Scandal?" Capisce was tossing the ball in the air and missing it, which made me feel better.

"Right. Yes, the 1919 Black Sox. And what happened to them? They were kicked out of baseball for life. Which they'd probably do to us, you know, keep us out of every park in the country, for life. That's after we grow old in prison and our families no longer talk to us."

"Well, then I agree with Tags, we keep our mouths closed." Lights stood and placed his right hand palm down near me.

"I agree, too. We say nothing, nothing . . . for life." Paulie got up and put his hand over his brother's. "I'd hate to get old sittin' in a stinkin' prison. Plus, I heard the food's lousy. What about you, Capisce?"

"Nothin' means nothing, right? Not even between only us can we say anything?" Capisce still lay on his back.

Paulie and Lights looked at me as if the whole situation had turned incredibly complex and hopeless. They pulled their hands from the swearing circle as if a fire had been lit below them.

"As long as we keep it to ourselves, I don't see a problem, but only between us when we're alone. That means we never talk about it in school. Only when we're here, or sleeping out, or in your cellar. Know what I mean?"

God, I hoped they did. But looking in their faces at that moment, I felt like a lone survivor floating helplessly on the rough seas. I wasn't sure they did get it.

"Yeah, I guess Tags got a point." Capisce got up and thrust his hand into the swearing circle. "We'll be silent heroes, like heroes should be. We do our heroic deed, then ride off into the lonely sunset as townsfolk turn and whisper to each other, 'Who were those masked men?'"

The Beacons and I looked at each other, then at Capisce. He had his bear paw of a hand extended and his chest pushed out and eyes closed, a smile slowly spreading on his big face.

"You mow-ron," I said.

"Oh yeah, who's the mow-ron?"

"You're all mow-rons."

"Yeah, but we take after the King of Mow-rons, you."

"I told you I was a good teacher."

And with that we piled hand over hand in the swearing circle, laughing and swearing on our mothers' souls to never again talk about the big caper for as long as we lived. We broke hands, picked up our gear and headed home with our spirits high.

I breathed in the cooling air, listening to the guys talking statistics and playoff possibilities. Feeling good really wasn't a precise description of my emotions at that moment; it was more like feeling . . . older. That was it! I began feeling older. I was watching and listening to the guys walking taller, talking bigger. If it is possible that making a commitment made you grow up in five minutes, then I'm witness to that fact. We argued about the MVPs, Cy Young awards, cloning the right-handed Rifleman, and home-run champs all the way home, sounding somehow more mature in our talk. I tossed the ball straight up in the air while I walked and it landed in my glove without me moving much. Some things just stand to reason, and some things leave you no explanation. We walked the rest of the way in mature silence, a new chapter opening in our lives.

EIGHT

October came with the speed of a Rifleman fastball. It was the second day of the month with four games remaining. The Sox had lost the July ten-game lead and now sat in second place by a half-game. The ghosts of all the years past had again risen to join forces against the good fortune of our beloved team . . . to no one's surprise. As Capisce would say, "It's always something."

This year's something was really something. The one player other than the Rifleman they couldn't afford to lose for an extended period of time was L.C. But the Red Sox being who they are, well, that's exactly what happened. Louie Cardinale was placed on the disabled list for the month of September. The way he got hurt was just another chapter in the cruel history of the Boston Red Sox. It seemed L.C. was eating in a downtown Boston restaurant, when, while serving him a very expensive and delicious flambé dessert, the chef mistakenly poured brandy not only on the cherries jubilee, but also on L.C.'s right hand, and lit them both on fire. The doctors agreed the burn was severe enough for a three-week stint on the DL. While Louie Cardinale recuperated and the fans drank everything in every bar in Boston, the team seesawed with the Yankees for first. They were holding tight, but everyone was waiting for the other shoe to drop. And this weekend the shoe was going to either fall with a thud or slip quietly back on, because the Yankees were coming to town for a season-ending three-game make-or-break series. The fans weren't completely ready to jump ship, because L.C. was ready to come off the DL. The fans were hoping he'd be ready to explode right out of the box.

Tonight's game was first, though. The Sox had the Orioles in town for the rubber game of their three-game series, and they needed to win tonight to draw even with the Yankees, who had the night off. The Orioles, the American League's worst team, had managed to take the first two games, dropping the Sox out of first place and into a must-win game. If the Sox won tonight, then the three-game Yankees series came down to either playoffs or go home.

The town was buzzing with cautious anticipation. Fenway Park was sold out, L.C. was in the lineup, the Rifleman was pitching and promising to come back on three days' rest if the team needed him. We'd all been here before, though.

I rushed through dinner to meet up with the guys at the Beacons' house. Dad had a new contract with a sporting-goods chain, selling them the buttons for their softball league sponsored jerseys. That was going to be golden for me. I figured a new glove a year for life sounded like a fair deal. It being Thursday and a school night, I had only an hour before I had to be back home. I excused myself and promised to clean my room later.

Lights, Paulie and Capisce were quietly staring at the television in the basement when I bounded down the stairs. The game was just starting, and the guys looked as if the Sox had already lost.

"So, do we wait until they're in third place?" Capisce looked up at me, his head in his hands.

"If they lose tonight, we go in tomorrow." I sat in front of the television hoping against hope that they weren't going to lose.

"You kiddin'?"

"We really doing it?"

"Tags, don't lie to us."

"No, I'm not kiddin', Lights. Yeah, we are gonna do it, Paulie, and no, Capisce, I wouldn't lie to you."

"Knockout, but I hope they don't lose."

"I hear you, Lights. But if they do, we gotta be ready to go. This is the whole scenario: Say the Sox win tonight, which they will, then they'll be tied for first with three to play. But if they lose tomorrow against the Yankees, that would put them a game behind with two to go. We have to do something Saturday if that happens. But, if they lose tonight and then win tomorrow, they'll be tied for first with two games left. If that happens, we watch Saturday's game and do nothing. If they lose Saturday, then we fix Sunday's game if need be, then we hope the one-game playoff for the division is back at Fenway."

"Why don't we fix Saturday's game? Then we'll know they end at least in a tie after Sunday."

"Yeah, I thought of that, Capisce. We could, but it still means a playoff game. "

"We gotta do something, Tags. I thought that was to be the whole Plan. We just can't do nothing."

"I didn't say nothing. We just have to wait and see what happens tonight and then Friday night before we decide. If we don't wait, we could screw up the whole deal. Anyway, let's go over the Plan again, make sure it's perfect."

On the television screen, the Red Sox were taking the field. The cloned pitcher, Rifleman Winchester, started to trot in from the right field bullpen. I couldn't have cared less if the story was real or not about him being a clone, the guy could throw peas through metal, and that's all that mattered. Watching him walk confidently toward the mound, I had no doubt the Sox were going to win tonight. It was the same feeling I had that Saturday was going to be the day.

Paulie started. "We get to the ballpark before the National Anthem. . . ."

NINE

I think it was Saturday morning. I stared hazily at the time. The Red Sox wall clock read seven-forty-five. The clock's second hand was a miniature baseball that was tossed by a pitcher standing on a mound at twelve o'clock, then caught by a catcher at the six and relayed back to the pitcher. This morning it seemed as if the second hand's baseball was speeding past the numbers and moving faster and faster. I rolled onto my back and on top of Twotails. She hissed and shot off my bed. I closed my eyes and focused on what day it was. When I opened them again, I hoped my first guess hadn't been the right one. Maybe it was it still Friday, or Sunday morning, and all was knockout in Red Sox Nation.

I opened my eyes slowly; it was Saturday, no doubt about it, and all wasn't knockout in the Nation. The baseball on the clock zipped from pitcher and catcher and back. I thought maybe Mom had put a new battery in, like a super-titanium Eveready or something that kicked up the speed. I'd never seen the second hand fly like this, but I knew why. Thursday night, the Sox had won as I had expected. The Rifleman had tossed a seven-inning two-hit shutout and Louie Cardinale had returned with a single, triple and home run. With a scare from the bullpen, the Sox had held on to win, three-two. We were now tied for first with the Yankees. Friday night, the Sox had lost the first game of the three-game series and now were a game behind with two to play. They not only had lost Friday night but got crushed, fifteen-one, by the Yankees.

The hope we all clung to over the summer had been replaced by the usual fan grumbling after last night's game, as in "here-we-go-again," "what-did-I-tell-ya," "it-was-only-a-matter-of-time," and my favorite, "wait-'til-next-year." They would've been right-on with any of those complaints and without any arguments from me, except that I just didn't agree. What I had hoped for months ago was for the team to have enough wins for my Plan to be set in motion . . . and that's exactly what happened. But now that the day (Saturday) had arrived, my legs and arms felt like jelly and my eyesight had become blurry. This wasn't a good sign for someone who was hoping to be a superhero legend for centuries to come. I tried to blink away the blurriness and stretch through the shakiness, but all I managed to do was give myself cramps in my eyelids.

"Oh my God," I think I blurted out. This was totally new. The cramps were the worst pain I'd ever felt. Except for the time when I was six and Capisce pushed me out of the treehouse in his backyard and I broke my ankle, I have never felt like screaming to the heavens. One eyelid was stuck together, the other open. As when I broke my ankle, I kept my screams inside.

"Honey? You okay?"

No! I'm dying in here, I felt like screaming to Mom. I'm going to be a Superhero legend and my body is cramped up like an old-timer.

"Yeah Mom," I said, "just hit my knee on the dresser. I'll be fine." I'll be blind, but fine!

"Are you sure you're okay? I came up to tell you Lights is at the back door."

Ahhhh! "I'm coming down." One eyelid, the closed one, opened slowly. It felt like someone was prying it open with two sharp forks. I wanted to yell but held my breath and waited as patiently as I could for the cramp to subside. The open eyelid peeled back and relaxed just as the closed one finally relaxed open. I blinked away the leftover tightness and could feel the jellyfish sensation leaving my body. The superhero legend had returned.

My number 5 white home Red Sox jersey was on the pile of clothes on my floor. Today, Paulie and I were the home team against Capisce and Lights.

"Hey, Twotails, you think Robin Hood ever peed his pants?" She was so mad at me for rolling on her, she didn't even turn to look at me. "Nah, I bet he didn't."

It was normal to be nervous, wasn't it? After all, men who went to battle stayed pretty calm until the time came for the bullets to fly. All men were just men until they were faced with proving themselves. That's when the men were separated from the superhero legends. You never know, a superhero legend could be hiding in everyone. But I still wondered if normal humans had problems like I did.

We had a big day today, so I hurried through my chores and breakfast. Mom had left a note on the table, something about a button trade show she and Dad were attending. With Twotails at my ankles, I headed toward the back door with glove in hand and stopped at the Cleanerama. My glove had lost the new look and feel to it. I had solemnly sworn I would never allow the glove to get old. Now, as I turned it over and studied the dark lines of dirt and sweat stains that covered the leather, I figured, why not? I've always wondered about the full capabilities of the Cleanerama. I dropped the L.C. glove onto the conveyer and hit the start button. If Mom were here, she'd have my hide. I peered through the window of the machine. The rubber arm whooshed down from its hiding place and scraped the glove back and forth. It then dropped the glove gently into the furnace area. The rubber arms came up and lifted the glove in a vertical position. So far so good, I thought. As the light-bulbs flashed and the dancing animals pranced behind my closed eyelids, I wondered for a split second if my glove was going to look like a piece of bacon. The door opened. The smell of fresh new leather drifted to my nose. When I opened my eyes, my "new" L.C. glove sat in the Cleanerama basket as safely as a baby in a blanket. Steam drifted off the shiny black leather. I touched it carefully. The leather was warm and soft but dry. When I put it on, my hand felt as if it molded into the leather.

"Knockout, Twotails." The glove opened and closed in my hand with the easiest of motions. "Why didn't I think of this before?" I went through picking up invisible ground balls, reaching for line drives and catching pop-ups, slapping the palm of the glove after each catch. The leather was softer than when it was new.

"This glove will never get old. This is definitely knockout. Wait 'til I tell the guys."

≡

They were waiting for me on the back steps of the Beacons' looking combat ready. I forgot about my glove as soon as I saw their faces and concentrated on the task at hand. Capisce was standing in the middle of the yard with his Black Python Hilberto Otto bat and was taking some mighty swings at imaginary pitches; the way-too-big bat looked like a toothpick in his hands this morning. Was it possible Capisce had grown bigger overnight? I glanced over at Paulie and Lights, who were sitting on the back steps flicking each other's ears with their index fingers. They definitely didn't look bigger this morning.

"Where you been, Tags?" Paulie got lasties in as he flicked his brother's ear and darted away. "We're all dyin' to get to the Pit. We're teammates today, right?"

"Yeah, sorry I'm late, guys. Mom had me do things around the house. What time is it, Lights?"

"L.C. says it's eight-twenty-one."

"You want to flip here or at the Pit?" Capisce took such a massive swing, I could feel the air swoosh from ten feet away.

"At the Pit like usual, you dodo bird." Lights realized what he had said to Capisce and took off running out of the yard and down the street.

Capisce acted like he was going to run after him for a second and then stopped. "Ha, look at him bolt! He looks like hornets are after his scrawny ass." The three of us burst out laughing until we heard Mrs. Beacon.

"Peter Capiscio, watch that mouth of yours." Her face poked out from the open window above Capisce.

Capisce cleared his throat and looked sheepishly toward Mrs. Beacon. "Yes, ma'am, sorry."

Paulie and I did all we could to keep from laughing ourselves sick. I didn't know whether to hold my stomach or cover my mouth, so I did both.

"Your mother and father wouldn't like hearing that sort of language, would they?"

"No, ma'am."

My stomach was hurting so bad I didn't know how much longer I could hold out.

Mrs. Beacon continued. "I'll act as if that language never entered my yard, nor will it ever again. Isn't that right, Peter?"

"Yes, Mrs. Beacon. And I apologize again, Mrs. Beacon." Capisce's mouth muscles twitched from holding back his laughter.

"You boys go play now, and behave. I'll pray for you."

We all thanked her and ran out of sight before we either split our sides or wet our pants. It wasn't until we were at the end of the street that we collapsed on Mr. Riggleman's lawn. Seeing Capisce standing under the window in perfect gentlemanly fashion and say "Yes, ma'am" and "No, ma'am" was more than the mere mortal could take. Paulie took on his mother's role and I became Capisce until Riggleman's dog chased us off his lawn down the street and over the tracks.

"Damn dog," Capisce yelled after we were free and clear.

"Whoa, did you say damn? Mrs. Beacon! Peter Capiscio swore again."

Capisce smacked me in the arm. Even though the hit wasn't what he could've delivered, I got the message that enough was enough.

We made our way through the dump and saw Lights sitting next to the shed. He was leafing through one of the girlie magazines as if he were reading a school book so he didn't hear us coming.

Capisce lowered his voice to sound like an older man and yelled at Lights, "HEY YOU . . . PERVERT!"

Lights flinched so hard, the centerfold he was studying ripped completely free of the old magazine and flew into the air. My next-door neighbor, Mrs. Emory, better known as Ms. April, 2009, went floating away on the cool October morning breeze. She drifted well in the breeze and disappeared over the heaps of metal corpses into the dump and dense brush. It was a humongous loss for all of us.

"Now we're even." Capisce lifted his arms over his head in victory pose.

"Geez, man, wasn't that Ms. April?" Paulie stood motionless, staring at the pile of junk as if it would toss back at us Mrs. Emory/Ms. April 2009, who was wearing, as my dad would say, something that would put him out of business.

"As I live and breathe. Yeah, anyone but her." It was a terrible loss. She had been a favorite of ours the day we found the magazine because we knew Ms. April 2009, knew her like our own mothers. Well, not exactly like our own mothers—our mothers would never take their clothes off in a magazine. She was like our mothers in age only, and mostly because she lived next door to me. Ms. April 2009 was Kelly Watters, Belmont High School, class of 2005. She married a few years after graduating, became Mrs. Emory, had four kids and unfortunately became a lot like our mothers as the years passed. Still, even though she was Mrs. Emory, to us she'll forever be Ms. April 2009, who just happened to be wearing nothing but a smile.

"Did you lose Ms. April 2009, you dolt?" Capisce's face scrunched up.

"If you didn't go scare me to death, I wouldn't have."

"Go get her."

"We'll all go get her."

"Let her go, guys." They all turned to look at me. "She deserves to be set free. We'll always have the memory of her right here." I tapped my forehead. "Plus, I'll always have the opportunity to see her out my window."

Capisce pointed toward me. "Get him."

Capisce, Paulie and Lights sprinted after me, but the minute we stepped onto the Pit, the memory of Ms. April 2009 vanished into thin air the way her picture had.

"Who flips? Paulie, get over here and flip."

So we played ball in the cool October air. With our futures and that of our beloved Boston Red Sox on the line later that day, we played like crazed kids playing their last game. We played hard, without the usual ribbing. We played focused. And we played as if we'd never play again.

Lights' L.C. wristwatch told us it was twelve o'clock as Capisce walked to the plate. With a seven-run lead and two outs in the bottom of the inning, he was most likely the last batter. I wanted to get Capisce to pop it up, so I decided to throw him an inside screwball that I knew was his weak spot; he just couldn't hold off the inside junk. Plus, with the breeze, a curve or screwball or a slider, if it caught the wind right, would break nicely. When the pitch left my hand, it had a perfect left to right rotation, just biding its time to bite and ride in tight on his wrists. Except halfway to the plate, the ball stopped breaking. The ball's rotation stopped, and it hung out over the middle of the plate with a "hit me" sign gift-wrapped around it. Capisce's eyes grew so big, I could see the reflection of the ball in them. He unleashed The Black Cobra from the tip of his right ear with such a swoop that I thought Hilberto Otto himself stood in front of me. A huge "unhhhh!" from the belly of Capisce belched forward as the Cobra connected with a resounding pop that sounded like a firecracker. The ball rocketed in a line over my head. I swear I smelled the tape burning as it passed. It kept going to the deepest part of right center, gaining height and distance as it traveled. No one moved; we all watched in awe as the ball lifted higher and higher and farther, clearing the tops of the right-field trees with ease and disappearing well into the brush. None of us had ever seen a shot like that, and from Capisce, of all people. It must have been a full thirty seconds before any of us could make a sound, and then it sounded like a farm of pigs and cows.

"Whoa-ho-ho," was my input.

"Keewupahhh," added Lights.

"Ahhrrlll," Paulie sang.

Capisce dropped—no, rather stylishly flipped—The Cobra away, and trotted slowly around the bases, pin wheeling his right arm as he went. He'd deserved to showboat with a home-run shot like that; it was monumental. As we grunted in unison, he landed with a super-duper-heavy double foot stomp on home plate, and not one of us razzed him. We actually swarmed him with high-fives and slaps on the back; he might've been the opposition for the day to me, but he still was one of us. We picked up our stuff and headed away from our own Fenway.

The game was over without the ball, and as we left, a silence and heaviness overtook me. I took one long look at the wall and what we'd built and accomplished all by ourselves and knew even this was going to get old some day.

"Game's over, isn't it guys?" I didn't look in their faces but I knew they knew what I meant.

TEN

The Red Sox game started at four o'clock. If we left at one-thirty and took our time walking the tracks, we'd get there in plenty of time for a world's famous sausage.

"Kinda like our last meal, right, Tags?" Capisce walked beside me tossing his tennis ball in the air and catching it behind his back with one hand; the guy had some hands.

"Such negative vibes, Il Capiscio? No, I see it more as a treat before our heroism."

We were dressed in our blue Red Sox jerseys. I wore L.C.'s 5 CARDINALE. What else would I've worn to pull off the greatest caper in history except the jersey of the greatest Red Sox player of all time? I also had my pockets stuffed with different-sized buttons to pull off the job—skinny, fat, large, small, smaller, round and flat. We were covered just in case the camera's size or angle had changed. The thickness of a quarter would probably do the trick, I figured, so I loaded up on the buttons that were about that thickness. I particularly liked the blue ones, the color was fitting, and the smoothness of the button was like a worn stone.

"Let's go see if we can see Ratso." Lights ran ahead and waited for a Capisce throw; he landed a perfect eye-level toss.

"Maybe on the way back."

"Then let's go over the Plan once more. Whatta you say, huh, Tags?" Paulie stopped walking and sat on the railroad track. "I'd like to hear it one more time, you know, just to make sure."

"Not a bad idea. I'd like to hear it too." Lights came forward and sat next to his brother.

Capisce made it unanimous with a sigh. "Why not, we got a few minutes." He tossed the ball about fifty yards up track and watched it bounce to a stop between the railroad ties about thirty yards farther. He sat and stretched his legs.

The sun had warmed the day nicely, the early morning cool replaced with the waning heat from a soon-to-be-missed friend. The sun changed your outlook on things when it slept for the winter, I thought sadly, things that we naturally took for granted. Like lying in the grass for hours, eating fruit right from the trees, walking the railroad tracks, running from Ratso through the tunnel, and baseball. We owed all these joys to the departing summer. I stretched toward the soothing heat. Soon enough, I groused to myself, we'd be sitting in the Beacons' cellar wondering what to do next. If things would just stay the same, we'd have forever to get the Red Sox their much-deserved championship. The idea about things eventually getting old crept back into my brain and I pushed it away.

I didn't want to, but I turned my face away from the sun and sat with my friends. Something felt very right about the moment as I joined them; we were board members at the most important company meeting we'd ever have in our lifetime.

"This is the deal . . ." I began.

We sat on the curb, sandwiched between two cars, directly across the street from the Green Monster. This was the day to treat ourselves to individual world's greatest sausages with the works. Most of the works, mustard, relish, onions and peppers, covered each of us, but we didn't care. The sausages tasted better today than ever.

"Oh, man," Lights commented, "it is our last meal. Even Capisce knows it."

Capisce pretended to tighten a noose around his neck. "Aaaah, water, water."

I almost choked laughing and noticed there was mustard all over my glove. "Cool it, Lights. Here, look, mustard for later." I pointed to my just-cleaned-but-soon-to-be-getting-old glove and the mustard. "See, we still haven't had our last meal."

"Very funny. We going in or aren't we?" Lights made the mistake of standing in the way of the stampede of people and got pushed away from us by the crowd. I got a quick glimpse of his hand in the throngs of people before he was devoured by the moving mass of people.

The excitement around us hung heavy, bordering on hysteria and close to being out of control. The police had stopped traffic on Lansdowne Street hours ago, leaving the street open only to foot traffic. It reminded me of the start of the Boston Marathon where thousands of runners walked shoulder-to-shoulder for a mile before they separated. The fans here weren't as orderly, bumping and hustling for position without a single "excuse me." The whole scene might have looked chaotic and void of manners, but somehow it was working. I'm not sure if this was a bad thing. I was just sorry I happened to be in their path . . . like Lights.

I noticed most people carried cameras, gloves, pennants, "number one" red and blue foam fingers, and food and drink. They were all ready to celebrate, and we were here to oblige them. The streets were alive, the fans vibrating like the skin on a snare drum. I didn't want to be here in their path, but I wouldn't have traded it for a zillion bucks. I glanced up at the big green wall and the net and felt as if I could leap over it with a single bound like Superman and land with a killer hook slide across home plate . . . L.C. style!

A large red Cadillac was parked above our entrance into Fenway, blocking it from view. It was time.

"We all thought you were a goner for sure. Got the time?" I had to yell over the crowd noise at Lights. He had mustard stains and dirt matted on him, and his face had a strained look, but he never looked happier to see us, regardless of the reason. I couldn't recall if he had come with a cap, but he didn't have one now.

"I thought I was a goner too. Those people are nuts. Tags, if the Sox win, I don't think I want to be around here. They're ready to explode."

It was fifteen minutes to game time. "We should get going," I said.

With Capisce in the lead, we made our way across Lansdowne Street. He was the muscle, the manhole cover man. As soon as he was under the car, I was to count to fifteen, then slip under the car and into the open manhole to the ladder. Paulie was to wait and count to thirty after I was in, in case there was trouble so we didn't bang heads while I was scampering out. Lights was next, thirty seconds after his brother, then Capisce in last.

≡

The four of us stood at the bottom of the ladder, closed in from the noise and confusion of what was taking place above our heads. I think the four of us felt the same; the noise and confusion were a lot more welcoming than the quiet sound of distant water dripping.

"Tags?" Lights whispered in my ear.

I jumped a mile. "Don't do that, you dolt! You scared me half blind."

"I was wondering about something." Lights' look was one of pure fright, like when you knew you did something that was going to get you in big trouble. "If one of us gets caught, or two of us, or even three, but one of us gets away, should we tell on the one or ones who didn't get caught?"

Well whatta you know, I thought, that was a doozy of a question.

"Of course not. Whatta you think, we're gonna rat on each other?" Capisce had answered it for me.

Truth was, it really didn't matter. Once our folks found out, they'd put two and two together and before you could sneeze, we'd all be singing like canaries. "Well, I wouldn't call it ratting, I'd call it sticking together, you know, like brothers."

"No, I call it ratting, squealing, or givin' up your brothers." Capisce's face was turning beet red.

"I dunno, Capisce." Paulie looked at Lights and me. "I figure we're in this as a team, we go down as a team."

"That's what I figured." Lights scratched his head.

"Me, too." Paulie scratched his head too.

"That's a majority. If one gets caught, we all get caught." I stuck my hand out and we met in a one-for-all, all-for-one handshake, except for Capisce. "C'mon Capisce, no one says we're gonna get caught. The fact is, we won't. It's just in case, you know, band of brothers sort of thing."

Capisce looked disgustedly at us. I know he must've been wondering what had he done to deserve these guys. He grunted but thrust his hand into the group. "I tell ya, you guys are major-league weenies.Who gets caught, I get to smash 'em before the cops can protect him."

"Sounds fair to me. Sound fair to you, Paulie?"

"Yup."

"You, Lights?"

"I don't want . . ."

"Lights, sound's fair, doesn't it?" I gave Lights a look he understood.

"Really fair, yeah."

"Then it's a deal, we all get the firing squad and Capisce gets to squash us." We split our group hand shake. "We should leave our gloves here in case we gotta bolt." The guys piled the gloves on the ladder rungs for a quick exit. I looked in the eyes of my friends and gave them the thumbs-up. "Well then, knockout . . . let's go. "

It felt much cooler down here than on our first visit, almost like a refrigerator or a tomb. I shook those thoughts from my mind, trying to keep my attention on the task ahead and staying very close to the damp wall. Looking at all the plaques, there were so many reasons hanging on these walls to validate what we were doing. We had to pull this off for the hundreds and hundreds of baseball players that had worn the Red Sox uniform, the players who had given everything but failed at the end: Raditz, Williams, Martinez, Pesky, Conigliaro, Yastrzemski, Clemens, Rice, Ruth, and Cardinale.

It was worth the life sentence we were going to get. And the notoriety. I could envision all the Red Sox, past and present, stopping by the jail to say hello, signing my jail-cell wall and giving me the thumbs-up for being the best fan of all time. There probably would be movie deals, book deals, personal appearances, maybe even parades. The more I thought of it, the more it made sense to get caught. If we got away with it, we were sworn by our solemn promise to keep our mouths shut. But if we did get caught, would the league take away the championship on some technicality?

Did the King of England insist that Robin Hood and his band of men return the stolen money to the rich? Of course not, but these were modern times, with modern stupidities. These were questions and dilemmas that faced leaders, and like Robin Hood, only time would recognize our band of heroes.

The faint squeal of a rubber tire on wet cement caught my attention. I put my finger to my lips to keep the guys quiet so I could listen. The hum of a motor going faint accompanied the squeak of tires. I got a whiff of a cigar, so I figured it was the wheelchair guy heading upstairs.

The door to the computer and the Brain was open a crack.

"Stay here for a second. I'm gonna go check to see if the guy's gone." The odor from the cigar hung like a heavy reminder of where we stood, right in the crosshairs of a sniper's gun.

"Shut up!" My cowardly inner voice spoke.

"Who shut up?" Paulie asked.

"Yeah, who?" Lights echoed.

"No one. I was talking to myself." I mumbled.

"Weird stuff, Tags," Paulie snorted.

"Oh, you never talk to yourself?" Capisce asked Paulie.

"He talks to himself all the time," giggled Lights.

"No, I don't, you dolt."

"I've never heard him," Capisce added.

"Yeah you do."

"Na-aah."

"Ya-aah."

"You guys," I whispered, "please!"

I left to check if the coast was clear. I knew being in a sniper's scope was cake compared to having to listen to them bickering. They were silent when I returned. "The coast is clear. Are you guys ready to make history?" Without waiting for an answer, argument, question, moan, groan, sneeze or burp, I pushed open the door to the room.

From inside the small room, the yelling of the fans sounded like we were under water. They sounded zany, but just being able to hear something gave me the feeling of being a part of the group. The room looked the same; computer wires dangled, hung, and looped, were flung, tossed, and dropped. The first thought that struck me was why the guy in the wheelchair didn't get all tangled up in the wires when coming and going, but then again, maybe he did. The camera—the Brain—was on its table-top tripod and pressed against the small plastic window. It was going through its warmup exercise, rotating slowly left and right, up and down, testing its field of vision. We watched like seasoned pros, having seen the routine before.

One thing I hadn't noticed the last time, though; there were tiny points, markings on the plastic window that looked as if they represented a perfect square box. Directly in the middle was a dot that I figured was the exact middle of the square, or what most likely represented the catcher's mitt in the center of the batter's strike zone. The camera was centered on the dot, and the lens could follow the degrees within that computer-generated strike zone. Tilt the tripod an eighth of an inch, and presto, a brand-new strike zone. The thinner, flatter blue button would have to be the one we used. I decided to put one under the right front leg of the tripod for a lefty batter, and one under the left for a right-handed batter. Simple. The only, well, maybe not the only, but the one hangup I had been messing with was when to upset the strike zone, and then how to remove any evidence that it had been disrupted. Doing it was never the problem, timing was the problem. But maybe I was getting ahead of myself; most likely the game would dictate the "when."

The camera stopped rotating and settled in the middle of the window, the lens extending to rest a hair away from the dot in the center. It was as if a fire-breathing dragon were ready and holding vigil.

The guys looked at me. "Now what?"

"We wait," I answered to no one in particular. "One of us should keep an eye out down the corridor just in case."

"C'mon, I know who you're gonna make keep watch," Lights quietly groaned.

"We'll all take a half an inning." I thought that was only fair. "Whatta you say?"

"Yeah, yeah, that's knockout," Lights beamed.

"Good show, 'ol chap," Capisce nodded.

"Buck-up first, then flip for firsties?" asked Paulie.

We all agreed. On the first buck-up I tossed in one finger and the guys did two; I was out on one exchange, no need to flip. They finished bucking up until we all had our innings determined. We were to rotate; I had the first, third, fifth, seventh, and . . . "Oh damn, I got the ninth-inning lookout."

"We all have to suffer, Tags," Capisce said sarcastically.

"Yeah, I'm sure."

I sulked out to the tunnel to keep watch. "Just keep me posted on what's going on." I looked over my shoulder at them all huddled close to the tiny window and the view of history possibly being made, and I hoped for my sake nothing happened, at least not until the bottom of the first inning. "And make sure you don't hit the camera, you dolts."

≡

"First and third, Tags, two outs, no score. Walker's not lookin' too sharp," Paulie whispered.

"Walker's a bum, I've been telling you that all year," Capisce added.

"He's gotten no run support, that's his problem."

"He's got a five-fifty earned run average, Lights. This ain't football, he should be better than thirteen and eleven with that kind of run support," Capisce snorted.

"Yeah, but remember at the beginning of the year when he was seven-and-one and had no run support, he practically carried the team."

"No, no, no, the Rifleman carried the team . . . oh shoot!" Capisce yelled.

"What? What? Tell me." I poked my head in, forgetting about my sentry post.

Lights looked at me like his pet had died. "Kyle Petrol just hit one into the screen. Three to nothing."

"Walker should be pulled, and now," Capisce said.

The Red Sox and Walker had got out of the inning behind three to zip. It wasn't the end of the world, but with the fragile state Red Sox fans were in, it wasn't time for celebration either. The fans tried to get the Sox into it but the Yankee's best pitcher, Tommy DeLand, whiffed Wallace, Henry and Palagrini. It was the start we'd prayed wouldn't happen.

Walker walked to the mound in the top of the second inning, greeted by boos. One thing about the Red Sox fans, what's happening right now overrules long-term devotion. When Walker struck out two of the three batters in the inning, I could see the fans behind home plate and on the first base line giving him a standing ovation; I guess living for the moment isn't all that bad.

"Tell me how L.C. does." It was Lights' turn to keep watch. "Every pitch, I want to know every swing."

Louie Cardinale strolled to the plate. The muffled cheers gave me goosebumps. I looked at Capisce, and he seemed to be holding his breath. "It's only the second inning, bro, relax." I wish I felt what I preached. The truth was I was holding my breath, too.

"He's hot, Tags. I'm thinking round-tripper, a dinger, a blast, an L.C. moon trip." Capisce lightly smacked Paulie.

"Yeah, yeah, me too." Paulie got in good position to see out.

Outside, ball one. "Ball one, outside," I relayed to Lights.

"Outside? They're pitching him away," Lights said.

Inside, ball two. "Inside, bawwwwlll two," I reported.

"Don't want to give L.C. anything good, can't say I blame 'em," Lights whispered from the door.

Ball three outside, and ball four inside. L.C. trotted down to first base with the first Red Sox runner. Now we were cooking with gas, I thought. Rally up the troops and watch out Jan-keys, here come the Bosox.

"Knockout! My man is up . . . Hilllll-berrrr-towww," Capisce squawked. "Bring 'em in, baby."

Otto swung at the first pitch—a six-four-three double play. Even the greenest of rookies knows to take a pitch after the pitcher walks the previous batter on four pitches. I felt like screaming out loud, "What the heck is he thinking!" but was afraid Capisce would squash me like a rotten peach. Two words of advice around Capisce—you never make fun of his size, and you never bad-mouth Hilberto Otto. I bit my tongue and looked at him; he stared quietly out the window and I swear there was steam coming out of his nostrils.

I broke the dead calm. "Okay . . . that's okay. Let's go, Lozaino, get something going."

Nothing got going, and after two innings the Yankees kept the three to nothing lead.

I paced the hallway during my watch in the top of the third. It was definitely too quiet out here so I poked my head in to get an update—two Yankee base runners, first and third with two outs.

I left to pace once again. As my dad would say, the day wasn't starting out as a "get-at-it-day." C'mon Sox, I thought, don't do it to us again, not this year, not the year of the best summer I've ever had.

"Tags? Where are you, Tags?" Lights came scooting out of the room like his hair was on fire. "We got out of the inning, still three-zip. Keep me up-to-date on what's going on."

Dupree opened the bottom of the third with a double off the wall that just missed being a home run. "I can't tell you how many times that left-field wall takes away home runs," I could hear my dad say. "More times than it gives you home runs," he'd answer himself. "They should rip it down." A fact he might be right-on with, especially hurting line drive hitters like L.C. But there was always something magical about watching a flyball falling into the big net above the wall. We were crossing our fingers hoping the Sox could get a rally going as Telinger strolled to the plate. Four pitches, and Telinger walked to first.

"Big rally, guys, I can feel it." Capisce crossed himself and looked accusingly at Paulie and me. We crossed ourselves without blinking and stared out the window. "Hey, it can't hurt, guys, can it?" Capisce didn't want an answer, didn't need one.

Could it be a get-at-it-day after all?

Maybe things were going to turn for the better after all. Steve Berano, the Sox catcher and ninth hitter in the lineup, ripped a single to left, bases loaded, no outs.

"Way to go, Berrr-annn-oo!" I slapped Capisce on the back. "Sorry, old pal."

"Save ya sorry's. Way to go, right on." Capisce did a little jig and crossed his fingers for good luck.

"Oh man. C'mon, Wallace, bring 'em in, you Hal, bring 'em in." Paulie copied Capisce's jig as Yankees' pitching coach Popeye Roker walked slowly to the mound.

"They're gettin' to him now, leave him in, coach." I looked at the fans through the tiny window. Most were standing in anticipation. Hal Wallace was a good leadoff man, good contact, good eye, good speed, not great, but quick enough to stay out of the double play. "Good eye, baby, good eye. He's no pitcher, no pitcher." Talking it up in baseball sounded so stupid if you really listened, but who listened? The idea was to distract the other team with senseless words and noises and confuse them. The guys caught on.

"Rubber-arm, Leee-land." Paulie added.

"He's no pitcher, just a belly-itcher." Capisce chimed.

"You call that a fastball?" I said.

"You couldn't pitch for our Little League team." Paulie laughed.

"Make that our Pee Wee team." Capisce slapped me on the back and nearly broke my shoulder blade.

"Ohh, hey, Wallace is up."

Lights stuck his nose in the room. "What's goin' on? It sounds like the ceiling's gonna come down."

His brother filled him in. "Bases pickled, no outs. We'll keep you posted . . . now keep watch."

Where I heard the saying, 'glory turned to tragedy,' I'm not sure. But it happened, and it happened quickly. Why Wallace picked on the first pitch, I'll never know. He hit a perfect five-four-three double play. It was perfect if you were a Yankee fan. The Sox did get one run out of it, but it left me with half-full feeling, like not getting your order of fries with your hamburger.

The next batter, Henry, struck out and the inning ended; Yankees 3, Sox 1. It wasn't exactly tragic, I know, but boy, it could've been really something.

The fourth, fifth and sixth innings topped the frustration meter like no other time in Red Sox history, if that's possible to believe. Except for a minor two-out rally by New York in the fifth, Walker had shut down their offense. It was the Red Sox lack of clutch hitting that had us ready to riot. The Sox left two on base in the fourth inning. They left the bases loaded in the fifth (L.C. popped out to end the inning, ahh)! And they left two runners in scoring position in the sixth. The Yankees' relief pitchers were walking the tightrope but the Sox couldn't knock them off.

We all thought the same: How often could you let these chances go by without taking advantage? Each of us was trying not to cast D-O-U-B-T over our party, but you might say we weren't holding it in well. You might say we were a bit fidgety. Or as Capisce called us, "girls caught out in the rain."

"If we're the girls, you're Mother Hen!" Paulie responded.

"Guys, don't start now," I cringed at the thought of a fight of words at this moment.

"We're getting toward showtime."

"Don't worry, Tags, I'll just wait 'til later . . . then I'll squash him."

"C'mon Tags, he started it. You heard him."

"C'mon . . . he started it." Capisce mimicked Paulie.

"Guys, if we pull this off, we're going to be heroes, real bigger-than-life, American heroes. The press will probably want interviews, pictures, stories of our lives." I looked at them with my arms spread and eyes wide.

"What's that got to do with the price of bologna?" Capisce said.

"Tea. The saying is, price of tea, ya big galoot." Paulie snorted.

"Oh boy, that's it, you're . . ."

"Bologna, tea, what does it matter? What matters is we act grown-up. That's what it's got to do with, that's what this whole thing's got to do with. Who cares who started it, or who said what, or who did what? It's time . . ." I ran out of stuff to say.

"Yeah? Time for what?" Capisce looked at me cross-eyed.

"Time for me to keep watch." There, that was good enough.

"Capisce, Capisce?"

"Not really. Matter-of-fact . . ."

Lights came bursting into the room, his words spilling out of control. "SomeonescomingIheardsomeonecomingwe'redeadreally screwednow."

"Whoa, Lights, slow down. Someone's coming? Are you sure?" I pleaded for some calm.

"Yeahyeahyeah someone's I heard thebellontheelevator."

"Whatta we do, Tags?"

I pushed past Lights and Capisce to the hall and heard a faint electric hum coming our way. "Out now, guys. Go toward the ladder . . . but be quiet." They ran out with me a few steps behind. Then it struck me; I couldn't remember if the computer room door was open or closed when we came. The guys were ahead of me and rounding the corner when I stopped. I turned around and came face to face with the wheelchair guy. Everything in my body stopped being my own; I was a paper cutout and the real me was over in the safe dark corner staring at my silly cartoon drawing. I think my brain was going to say something like, "I'm lost. Aren't those world famous sausages delicious?"

My jaw dropped as the wheelchair guy disappeared into the tiny room. I was frozen; how could he have not seen me? A miracle? A miracle like the Red Sox winning the World Series? I didn't want to push my luck. I found my insides to go with my body and ducked around the corner. The guys were probably halfway home. Whatever happened to all-for-one-and-one-for-all?

Capisce whispered into my ear. "You get him?" Behind him, shaking, were Lights and Paulie.

"I knew you guys wouldn't leave me." Yeah right, I thought.

"Yeah right." Capisce patted me on the head.

"The wheelchair guy's in the room. He went right by me without seeing me. Now I know the Red Sox have a chance. It's like a miracle."

"We wait, or should we go?"

I was about to say, "I dunno," when the hum of the electric motor broke my thoughts. I heard it low-like, as if the guy was creeping out of the room. The hum stopped; the quiet caught us unprepared. I motioned to the guys to back up slowly. What was it? What got the man's attention? We left the door wide open, didn't we, I thought? Or did I close it tight?

Oh God, our gloves! I couldn't remember whether the door was open or closed, but I knew we'd left the gloves at the entrance to the manhole, my idea, I recalled. We back-stepped very quietly, waiting for the hum of the electric motor to close in on us. I couldn't believe this was happening. Thirty thousand fans above us, plus hundreds of thousands waiting around televisions and radios for the unbelievable to happen, for the Red Sox to actually BEAT the hated New Yawk Jan-kees, and we were being held hostage by a fat guy in a wheelchair. Time was running out—it was the seventh inning when we ran out of the room with the Red Sox losing, three-one. Three minutes ago a miracle was taking place, now a nightmare had replaced that. I couldn't let this happen. Twenty years coming after eighty-six years of such mistakes, bonehead plays, bad luck, umpires' calls, and curses . . . now this! No way!

If I was Robin Hood with his band of outlaws, then the guy in the chair was the evil English king coming to arrest us. The faces of the poor and needy of yesteryear came into my mind; the pain and the suffering would stop this year. We came to do a job and we will, I trumpeted to myself.

"He's coming," Lights shrieked.

"Oh holy mutha . . ." Paulie breathed.

He grabbed his brother's shoulder to pull him toward the ladder just as I grabbed Paulie's to pull him back. Capisce got stuck in the middle of this with a dumbfounded look that would've been hilarious in any other circumstance. My arm was around Capisce's back and gripping Paulie who had an outstretched arm holding his brother. Lights looked like Rubberband Man being stretched left and right. Capisce snapped out of his daze and started to push toward escape. His push broke my grip.

"Wait!" I yelled. Well, if the guy hadn't been coming, no doubt he was now. I could hear the hum of the wheelchair's motor getting louder. The guys stopped dead in their tracks and turned and stared at me with eyes that said, Are you crazy, man?

"This way," I blurted out and turned to face the oncoming army of one.

"We gotta skedaddle, Tags." Capisce said.

"Skedaddle? Who the heck says . . . ?"

I started down the tunnel. I really honestly, absolutely, and without a doubt in the world hadn't a clue about what I was going to do. What I did know was that it was way too late for us to skedaddle. I could hear one of the twins say something about dead meat. Perhaps, I guessed.

But what else would true heroes do but risk their own lives for those less fortunate?

I came out of the shadows to face my fate. I was so close to the guy I could smell the cigar smoke and beer on his breath. The guy had come down here to have a drink and a cigar. Oh boy, did we turn things upside down!

"What in the world are you doing down here?" he said with a rasp. His wheelchair stopped and began to go in reverse.

I choked on my words. I wanted to say to save The Red Sox Nation. I think I said your mother sleeps in a space capsule. Whatever I said, it didn't stop him. His chair was zooming backwards as if he was trying to outrun me . . . and believe you me, he would have if he hadn't backed into the open door and knocked himself out cold. (Oh yeah, I just recalled we had left the door wide open). The guy's chair hit the open door so hard his head had snapped back and whacked the edge of the thick door. He was knocked out before he could say "Ouch." His head had fallen forward and lay still on one of his chins against his stomach.

"Did you kill him?" Paulie stood a few feet behind me. He was breathing so heavy I could feel his breath on my neck.

"What'd you do, Tags, scare him to death?" Capisce said nervously.

"Life. We're in for life." Lights pulled on his brother's arm.

I stepped close to the guy and peeked under the bill of his cap. His eyes were shut tight. I figured that was good because most people when they died, died with their eyes wide open. I think they did, or do, or . . .

"Is he breathing?"

"I dunno."

"Check."

"How?"

"Anyone got a mirror? I've seen once, if you put a . . ."

"No one's got a mirror, Lights."

"Slap his face."

"What?"

"If he's alive, he'll come to. I saw it . . ."

"I'm not slapping him. You slap him."

"Not me."

"No way."

"Don't look at me."

"Toss a glass of water on him."

"You see anyone here with water?"

"I know, yell in his ear, if he's alive he'll flinch."

"Don't tell me, you saw that once?"

"Yeah, I think. Or maybe I did it to Twotails when I thought she was dead."

"Hey Tags, ya might have to do mouth to mouth on him."

What friends I had! As they stood behind me giggling like schoolgirls, my heart jumped.

"He's breathing," I croaked. One of his chins was going up and down on top of his stomach. I'll never swear again, God, I swear, I solemnly swore. The guy seemed to be out cold so we had to finish our job. I took his walkie-talkie out of his top pocket.

"What if he comes to?"

"First you want him to come to, now you don't want him to come to, make up your mind, Capisce."

He was right, though. If he did wake, he'd go get help. We'd have to, as they do in Army Intelligence, immobilize the enemy.

"Maybe we can back him up and lock him in the elevator?" Paulie suggested with a smile.

"Paulie, you're a little different, aren't you?" I stared at him.

"Duct-tape his mouth. That stuff holds space capsules together." Lights beamed with his thought.

"I would but I left my roll in my car." I shook my head in amazement; then it came to me.

"Capisce, give me a hand." In the back of the guy's chair was a battery, just like in a car. "When I unscrew this," I pointed to the screw that held the terminal wire, "slip it free. Got it?"

"You never stop amazing me, Tags-a-reeno."

I loosened the wingnut as Capisce yanked the wire free. "Back in business, gents. Paulie, just run down and see if the elevator is open or closed. This should hold the guy in place until we're finished."

Paulie ran back to tell us the elevator door was closed which I assumed for no particular reason was good. "That's good," I said.

"Why?" asked Lights.

I didn't even have a good lie. "We have to get back to the game." It seemed as if for a moment we all had forgotten the most important reason for being here, and then at once remembered.

The four of us charged into the room like a comedy act. Lights and Paulie locked shoulders at the door, Paulie finally popping free like a seed from a grape. Capisce gave us the news; top of the seventh, Yankees four, Red Sox one, two outs, runners on second and third. "They're finally pulling Walker. Looks like it's Brother's turn."

"Oh, Brother," the Beacons said together.

I had to agree with them on that one. Trent Brother was the Sox's lefty middle reliever who, for the second half of the year, stunk worse than a farm of skunks. The call could be heard in every corner of Red Sox Nation when he trotted in from the bullpen; "Oh Brother," I echoed. "Six point four-five ERA over the last twenty games," I recited. "Six homers, and about a hundred walks!"

It was still my inning to keep watch, so I started out to the corridor without arguing about the half-inning situation or any other half-baked reasons the guys could conjure up. "I'll be outside."

The wheelchair guy was still out cold. I noticed he had a name tag pinned to his collar but because of his chins I hadn't seen it before. "Well, Vince, the bums are blowing it again."

Paulie stepped to the doorway. "Brother walked Fernandez on four pitches." Oh Brother. "Bases pickled . . ." Oh Brother . . . "two outs, and Zeiker's up . . ." Oh Brother Oh Brother Oh Brother. "Looks like they're keepin' Brother in, you know, lefty on lefty." Paulie stepped in shaking his head.

I couldn't take it anymore. Zeiker was their best hitter. The heck with being caught.

"Don't go anywhere, Vince."

I darted into the room to join my brothers in agony. The four of us squeezed around the camera to get one eye on the action. First pitch . . . and here it came, high and long and directly at us . . . Oh Brother! Dupree's name on his back was getting larger and larger as he backpedaled toward us.

"Can you see it?"

"Where is it?"

"Is it gone?"

"Anyone see it?"

Dupree had disappeared from our sight. We all held our breath, waiting and waiting for the call. Please, gods of the baseball world . . . Don't do this to us! We can't take it anymore! I had to make sure I wasn't screaming and spitting all over the room.

"He's got it . . ." Capisce began to scream. "Dupree's got it, he caught it, over there, he caught it. He went up and over the bullpen. Knockout! "

We all joined in. "He caught it? Superknockout...Squared!" I added the squared, which after it came out of my mouth sounded a little wimpish, but luckily the guys were so happy they let that one slide. Dupree had faded into the corner of the centerfield triangle, four hundred twenty feet away from home plate, and thrown himself into the bullpen to make the catch. It was reminiscent of Dewey Evans' catch in the 1975 World Series, except Dupree landed in the bullpen and on his head. It was incredible. We watched in awe at the replay on the Jumbotron behind home plate. There were, and had been, so many ups and downs, twists and turns, not to mention flips and flops in the history of the Boston Red Sox, I wanted to believe that this catch could be the turning point for good fortune. But I think at that moment I realized what it meant to be a true Red Sox fan. Watching in quiet awe with my friends at Dupree's feet flying in the air, I knew we all loved to secretly suffer in our team's failure. Why else put ourselves through this for the last twenty years except for the pleasure of failure? Maybe it was just me, but it felt as if 35,000 fans wanted that ball to be a home run so they could be disappointed. The time was upon me, I thought justly, I'd become my father.

While the guys high-fived each other, I went out to look at Vince. The game was getting near the end. The season, another season of hope, was coming to another devastating close; I couldn't get soft now. Staring at Vince, I felt sadness, for him, for me, for us all. So many years. I'd watched my father turn from bleeding red and blue to watching occasionally to not caring. The past twenty years had sucked hope, the most important part, from my father's and the other fans' cores. Hope was ripped out like a bleeding, pumping heart, held up for show, satisfied for one year in 2004, and then dropped in the river of despair to float until another generation, waiting at river's end, rescued it and passed it on . . . then on . . . and on. . . .

"Hey, Tags," Paulie's voice snapped me alert. "The Sox got a rally going, first and second, no outs."

I bolted around Vince and into the room; I was a Boston Red Sox fan . . . again! "Who's up? Tell me L.C.'s up." Here we go again!

"Palagrini's up. L.C.'s on deck ready to take it, 'So long Every-boddddy.'"

"Good one, Lights, you banana head." Paulie flicked his brother's ear. "Don't curse them."

"Yeah, I know Paulie. I'm not cursing, I'm just sayin' . . ."

"Guys, they're leavin' in Tinsley to pitch to the Pal Man."

"They might have to, they're running out of pitchers."

"Oh, c'mon Pal Man, don't let us down." We started a two-word chant, a Zen mantra. "Pal Man, Pal Man, Pal Man, Pal Man, Pal Man, Pal Man, Pal Man, Pal Man."

And then the unbelievable happened; first pitch, home run, right field. Game tied up, four-four. We lost our minds. Our yelps and screams blended into a dance as the four of us bounced like we were on a trampoline. The walls and ceiling could've crumbled and we wouldn't have noticed, life would've still been grand. I tried to steer my friends away from the bundle of wires and cables . . . the war wasn't over just yet.

"He did it, man, he did it!" Paulie slugged Lights, who slugged me, and I slugged Capisce, who slugged Lights, and on it went until Lights noticed L.C. popping out to end the inning. They'd renewed our faith in 'da bums' once again.

"I knew they'd do it." Lights beamed.

"No doubt-ah-bout-it." I added.

"Did anyone think otherwise?" Paulie said.

"I can't take it. I don't care whose turn it is, I'll keep an eye on the door." Capisce walked out as if the ending had already been written.

ELEVEN

"I'm sorry if you hurt yourself."
Vince was awake. I tried to talk at eye level to him because I'd heard that was the proper way to talk to a person in a wheelchair. Plus, when word reached the streets, I wanted everyone to hear of our kindness and thoughtfulness. People loved Robin Hood.

"Are you thirsty?" Good one, I thought, except I didn't have anything for him to drink.

"Nah, I'm all right. What happened?"

"You bumped your head on the edge of the door. Are you sure you're okay?"

"Better than you kids when you get bagged. What're you kids doin' down here anyway? How'd you get in? Through the manhole, huh? I bet you got in through a manhole. I told Mr. Kendall . . . Hey, you better not be in that room. I'm the only one with access to that room." Vince tried to maneuver his chair, then realized he had no power.

"What if I shared a secret with you, Vince? But you have to promise not to tell anyone until after tomorrow's game. If you do turn us in before tomorrow, then I'll tell you've been drinking on the job."

"What is it that you think you're doing?"

"We're planning on stealing the game for the Red Sox." I spoke the words like a seasoned professional. "Too many heartbreaks and close calls. So, we're here to put a stop to the suffering the Red Sox fans have endured for the last twenty years. We'll be heroes, but most importantly, the Sox will be champions again."

Vince just stared at me, rubbing the back of his head. "You're gonna do what?"

"Steal the championship . . . if we have to."

"And how do you expect to do that?"

"I can't tell you yet, Vince." I wanted to, but thought if he knew before we pulled it off, it would mean bad luck, and the Sox didn't need any more of that.

"Bottom of the eighth, Tags," Capisce came out to tell me.

And so it went; bottom of the eighth, then the top of the ninth, then the bottom of the ninth. The Red Sox and Yankees, tied at four, bottom of the ninth.

Our time had arrived.

We decided to forget about watching the corridor for this inning; we agreed we all needed the team approach to the Plan.

"All for one, and one for all." Lights hit his brother, Paulie hit me, I tapped Capisce, Capisce slammed Lights.

"Ouch, c'mon, Capisce." Lights smiled at Capisce. "Hey, but I don't care."

"Here we go, guys. You all set?" We all nodded. Did it matter if we weren't? I was ready and that's all that mattered. We were about to change the new Curse . . . the course of history . . . forever.

I glanced at the guys, who stared unblinkingly out the tiny window. My heart skipped a beat. What was the future for each of us, I wondered.

"Tags? You with us, Tags? It's the bottom of the ninth."

I stared at Lights and noticed he had a snot bubble growing as big as a balloon. Capisce was twisting Paulie's earlobe and smiling approvingly at me; they were my twelve-year-old friends again, for now.

"Ready, Freddy." I took out my buttons of all sizes I'd brought from home. It was Showtime. I glanced at the guys once more and wanted to lock in our youth forever—snot-bubbles and all. "Let's see if we can bring home a winnah!"

The buttons I laid out next to the Brain alternated between paper, dime and quarter thickness. If my calculations were correct, the tiniest of alterations would alter the strike zone in our favor; it was time to experiment.

"Top of the order, Tags. What's your plan? Wallace leads off."

"This is how it's gonna go . . ."

And boy, did everything go knockout. I couldn't have imagined in my wildest dreams how perfectly my plan worked . . . right up to the moment the security officer busted our operation.

TWELVE

"Don't look back, Lights, just keep running."

The four of us hit the path leading to the railroad tracks. Capisce was up ahead and gone by ten lengths, followed by me, Paulie, then Lights. I was shouting not to stop, not to look back, when I realized my worst nightmare had become a reality.

I had left my new glove in the tunnel.

I stopped as if a brick wall had just appeared in my way. Paulie, right behind me, bowled me over and down the embankment on the other side of the tracks. I was in such shock from leaving my glove behind I didn't feel any pain. I landed with a crunch flat on my back staring up at the darkening sky. Paulie and Lights bent over me with their mouths opening and closing in unison but I couldn't hear a word. All I could think of was . . . my glove my glove my glove my glove my glove.

"Tags? Tags? Get up, Tags. The cops . . . Tags?"

"My glove! I left…My glove!"

I snapped alert and struggled to my feet.

"We all did. C'mon, we gotta go. Forget about the gloves."

"No, you don't understand. My father gave me that glove." Oops, I said it, just like in my dream. Right there, under the brothers' intense questioning, I spilled the beans like a broken prisoner. That's right, guys, my father bought the glove. My dad, because he loves me, I wanted to say now that I was looking at jail time, my father bought me a new glove. Go ahead, lay it on, sing a song about how spoiled I am—I can stomach the insults.

"We'll say it was stolen."

"Yeah, we'll tell your dad Ratso jumped ya and stole it right off your arm."

What? No insults, no songs? I wasn't prepared for their kindness. "Yeah, that's right," I blurted, "my father bought the glove."

"Whatever, we gotta get outta here."

"You guys coming, or you gonna stand there with your fingers up . . . ?"

"Tags left his glove back in the tunnel."

"We all did, but I'm not goin' back." Capisce had run back to see if we were all right.

"That's what we've been saying."

"I'll go back." Maybe I hit my head when I fell because I wasn't sure those words were coming out of my mouth. "I have to . . ."

"No way, Tags. We'll all tell your dad it was stolen. If we go back, we're fried. Right, Capisce?" Paulie looked nervously over his shoulder.

"Oh geez!" Capisce began bouncing, his eyes bulging from his head. He turned and bolted up the tracks so fast he kicked up a tornado of stones. "Run you guys, run . . ." he yelled.

We turned as a team, Paulie, Lights, and me, to look behind us. Two hundred yards away stood a dozen thousand policemen all pointing in our direction. Paulie, Lights, and me turned as a team once again and ran as fast and as hard as we ever had run in our lives.

The rocks laid out between the railroad ties aren't easy to balance on when running as fast as you can. So on days when we had nothing else to do, we practiced timing our running steps to hit the wooden ties instead of the rocks. If you could get your timing down, you could avoid the rocks and almost float across the train tracks. The trick was in focusing on the tie two steps ahead of your next step. We must've practiced more than I remembered, because the four of us looked like the United States Olympic track team.

"Get . . . off . . . at . . . the . . . tunnel." I yelled in between leaps.

The tunnel was Ratso's hole. The guys all knew what that meant; we were going to have to risk our lives in order to save our lives.

The fence that separated Belmont High School and the tracks had a barely noticeable slice in it that would lead us off the tracks and to a covered-over narrow path. You'd pass right by the path if you didn't know the fence was cut. The path hadn't been used for years, overgrown with thick brush because of the Ratso story. Since the day that half of Poor Percy Hill was discovered, kids would avoid walking by the hole in the fence because they were afraid of Ratso leaping out and making them his dinner. The path was perfect for our getaway, if it was still passable.

I could see the bend in the track and the corner of the high school. Fifty yards ahead was the opening in the fence and the path. If we made that corner and then the path, the cops following us wouldn't be able to tell where we got off.

I didn't dare look back, trying instead to concentrate on my footing. In my head I counted a cadence; one-two-three-four, one-two-three-four, again and again, over and over. When I glanced up, the guys were standing still on the opposite side of the hole in the fence, away from Ratso's tunnel, and away from our getaway! They were wildly waving me on.

"Go . . . in . . . I'll . . . be . . . right . . . there." I was less than fifty feet away.

Capisce grabbed Paulie by the arm and pulled him toward the fence. Paulie dug his feet into the rocks like a mule and yanked in the opposite direction. Lights grabbed his brother's free arm and pulled on it like a chicken bone. They danced a frightened ballet as I streaked by them and pushed through the fence. What I was doing, I did out of pure fright. The guys probably saw my act as heroic, a general leading his troops into battle. So be it, but I'll tell you I did it without thinking. I hit the fence and popped through because I was sure I could feel the cops' breath on the back of my neck. The worst to come couldn't be any riskier than what was behind me. Could it?

The path was so overgrown with vines I tripped not two feet in and did a header down the sloping path toward Ratso's tunnel. About twenty feet away from the hole in the fence I just came through I stopped, tangled up in a prickly bush. I could hear the rattle of the chain-link fence snap back like a hungry jaw three times; I prayed it was my friends. As they tripped over the same vine and landed on top of me, one by painful one, I could only think next time I'd be sure of what I prayed for.

"Get off of me, you bunch of apes."

"Get Capisce off of me."

"Move your foot and I will."

"If you didn't push me down the hill."

"Who you sayin' pushed you?"

"I saw you push him, Capisce. I was . . ."

"Guys, we don't have time, get me untangled." They did their best to free me as we expected to hear the cops coming down the path. "We have to go in, you know that." I looked at the three of them and they stared back without blinking. "It's either that," I pointed up the path, "or this." I pushed a few branches aside and there, beckoning, was Ratso Risoli's home.

"It's like the devil we don't know is better than the devil we know." Lights looked up the path, then at me.

"Couldn't have said it better, Lights."

"What if we just lay low, stay here until night?" Capisce pleaded.

"No way, uh-uh. I'm not waitin' for nighttime. Ratso will hear us, you know, the huge ears." Paulie covered his mouth as if Ratso stood beside him.

"I'm with Paulie, I'm not hanging around. If Ratso's around, I want to see him coming."

"I'm just sayin', maybe we don't have to go in the tun . . ."

We all heard the voices on the train tracks. And as one, we scrambled without thinking, over the bushes and into the dark entrance where Ratso Risoli waited.

THIRTEEN

The first few steps into the tunnel were the easiest. The daylight came over your shoulder and the entrance was slightly raised so you weren't standing in knee-deep water. Ratso didn't live here. He lived in the middle of the tunnel where the walls breathed and the water turned to acid. And where we were headed.

Now the water was up to our thighs and I couldn't see my hand in front of my face. The smell was awful, worse than dead fish. We all covered our noses and walked carefully, trying not to fall down into the stinking water. Moss grew everywhere, sometimes hanging from the ceiling and directly into our path. We knew that when it became darker, the hanging moss would feel like soft fingers across our skin. With Ratso lurking somewhere in the shadows, walking into the moss could give you heart failure.

"Why don't we wait here, then go out and around and get on Concord Ave? Whatta ya say, Tags?" Capisce whispered.

"That's too risky, and that'll take too long. We have to get home and over to the Beacons' house before the cops get there to make it look like we've been hanging around all day watching the game," I whispered back. "And the only way is this way."

"The only way?" Lights gulped.

"Unless you can think of another." They were silent. "Let's go in single-file. I suppose I'll lead. Who wants the end of the line?" After the usual griping, complaining, whining and "why do I have to," Paulie volunteered for the first half and I did for the last.

Ratso's tunnel was the water runoff from the stream behind the library on Concord Avenue and had an opening next to the Underwood Pool. The level of water in the pipe depended on the amount of rain we'd had. Hopefully it was only up to our thighs and not our necks, or worse. I couldn't remember if it had rained lately. I didn't think so, but . . .

We started slow, careful not to slip on the wet moss, walking as close together as we could without tripping over each other, in frightened silence. As the pipe became darker and the water colder and deeper, Capisce's idea of waiting and taking Concord Avenue seemed like a fantastic one. I pushed aside the slimy moss from my face and spit out the awful taste from my mouth. It was too late now to turn around because from the slope of the ground under my feet I could tell we were halfway home. The water for some reason started to feel warmer, maybe because it was runoff from the town swimming pool. For whatever reason, it made us feel calmer. We knew we were close to our escape.

Suddenly the calm turned to chaos. We heard the noise coming from the wall to our left. I held my breath and could hear Lights gasp in fright.

"Tags?" Lights grabbed my arm.

"You guys hear that?" Capisce whispered.

"What was that?" Paulie asked.

"I dunno," was my feeble response.

I did know, but my hopeful side said it was nothing.

Raspy breathing like a busted steam engine echoed from our left. The sound made my skin crawl. Forced, raspy breathing, the kind made by a monster with no face. Like the sound Ratso would make. We stood frozen in our steps, listening to the terrible sound and drip, drip, of water. I started to shiver. I reached out my hand in the dark and grabbed a handful of something slimy, wet, and cold. I tried to tell myself to run, to take off, but every part of me refused to budge. The breathing seemed to go on, but still no one moved. Ripples of water hit my shins and echoed off the far wall. It was all I needed to set myself in motion.

"Run!" The word flew from my throat as I picked up my soaked sneakers and hit the ground like a champion sprinter. Ratso was closing in on us.

"Run, and don't look back." I flew toward the light at the opening of the tunnel. "Hurry guys, we're almost there."

The guys hadn't wasted a breath. We scooted through the pipe like rocket men, slipping and sliding, screaming and hollering like we were on fire. If the cops were nearby, we were sure as the button on my shirt fried on the spot. "I see the opening . . . hurry."

The opening was getting bigger, the light brighter, the water warmer. My legs were getting heavier with each step but Ratso's breath on my neck kept my feet in motion. "Where's Ratso? Keep going . . . anyone see Ratso?"

The soles of my dripping sneakers hit the dry grass outside the pipe's mouth and I didn't stop running. I reached up and grabbed the cement wall to pull myself up and felt hands pulling on my shirt and me back into the hole. My feet were pulled out from underneath and I landed on my knees. I covered my head, ready and expecting Ratso to devour me for his dinner. Instead, I got a sneaker full of Capisce's weight directly in the middle of my back.

"You comin', Tags?" Paulie streaked by me with his brother.

Was I coming? I pulled myself up the wall with every ounce of strength I had left and bolted up the hill with my legs shaking. We were almost home and we'd pulled it off. I didn't allow myself to turn around and look back until I was standing at the top of the hill. The guys were already crossing the playground and heading toward the Beacons' yard when I allowed myself to look. My jaw dropped. A dark shadow slithered along the far wall at the opening of the pipe and then dissolved into the entrance. "Son-of-a . . ." I wheeled around to yell to get the guys' attention, but then thought better of it; it would forever be my little secret.

They'd never believe it was a true story, and as a matter of fact, I wasn't sure that what I saw really happened. I walked slowly across the playground, too exhausted to run. I must've looked like I had been through a war. But I'd say this turned out to be a "get-at-it-day," indeed.

FOURTEEN

For five days the four of us lived in constant fear of the knock on the door. When the weekend came and the coast was still clear, we figured we must've pulled it off. We honestly didn't know how. How come Vince hadn't turned us in? How come the gloves hadn't been found? We had done everything right . . . but we had done everything wrong.

"Did your dad ask about the glove?" Capisce was biting his fingernails as we sat around the Beacons' cellar pondering our good fortune and hoping it really was good fortune. "Because my dad was wondering about mine."

"Yeah, he asked me once but my mom interrupted with something about her work. He hasn't brought it up again." I was fiddling with the television. Our favorite old movie, Field of Dreams, blurred past us. The Red Sox were about to take the field at Fenway for the third game of the American League playoffs. Certain things were just more important at certain times.

"Geez, Lights. When are your folks going to get a new television?"

"Tell me about it."

"What did your dad say about your glove?" Paulie asked Capisce.

"He was curious because he's so used to seein' me carrying it everywhere. I told him I put it away for this year. I think he was a little suspicious, you know, with the Red Sox in the playoffs and all.

He expected the glove to be glued to my hand. What about your parents?"

"They never asked," Paulie answered.

"I've been wondering why the cops never brought the gloves by; they had our names on them. You think they never found them?" I finally got the picture in clear on the television and settled into the sofa. The guys were unusually quiet as I looked and studied their faces. They all stared at me with puzzled expressions.

"You had your name on your glove?" Capisce asked in disbelief.

"No way." Lights followed.

"Get outta here," Paulie finished.

"Yeah, I wrote it on the thumb. It was new, so . . . what, you guys didn't?"

"I did when it was new, yeah, but it wore off years ago."

"Me too. When we got our gloves, Lights and me both put our names in them. Mine was worn off, too."

"I never did." Capisce pointed at me. "But if you had, how come we didn't get caught?"

"I have no idea, unless they weren't found. But I can't believe that. We left them . . ." Then the reason hit me, at least a good explanation.

"What, Tags? You look like you just saw the Red Sox win The World Series," Capisce laughed.

"The Cleanerama!" That must've been what happened. I nodded. "The Cleanerama must have washed my name off. I never noticed or thought of looking."

"You put your glove through the Cleanerama? Knockout. How'd it come out?"

"Came out great, Lights. We didn't get caught!"

We broke into nervous laughter and settled in to watch the Red Sox. Twotails had nosed her way through the open cellar window and now rolled in front of us with her legs in the air. Her belly was covered with bits of leaves, and wrapped around her front paw was a white string. We all looked at her in quiet fascination. At the beginning of the summer we wouldn't have been able to suppress our hysterics at the sight of her. But sadly, the summer was over. And with the passing of the season, we'd become hardened, more tempered, and perhaps a bit older.

EPILOGUE

Now, to continue the story would be inappropriate. The story and the summer were about our youth, thirty summers past, where diamond dust, Red Sox batting averages, fastballs, and Louie Cardinale meant the world. It was the last summer we played at the Pit, the last summer we hung out at the dump, and the last summer little things didn't bother us. Remember us with dirt on our faces and an attitude. We smelled of cut grass and existed for only one thing, baseball.

I haven't seen my buddies in some time. I used to watch Big Peter Capiscio on television wrestling under the name, "General Cap." I believe he held the championship belt for a year. Last I heard, he owned a wrestling school in Oregon.

Paulie moved to Florida after high school and became a horse breeder and owner of thoroughbreds. He even entered a horse in the Kentucky Derby. He invited me to join him in his owner's box at the Derby. That was the last I saw of him and his brother. Although his horse lost, we had a great time talking about the old times . . . and the Red Sox.

Lights worked with his brother for a while before finding a calling and becoming a minister.He's called the Reverend Joe Beacon, from Florida's First Church of the Light of God.

After high school I got a scholarship to play baseball at Boston College and actually got drafted by the, ahhh I hate to admit this, THE NEW YORK JAN-KEYS. Can you believe that, of all teams?

But as fate would have it, I blew out my pitching arm the first year in the minors and that was that. I never even tried a comeback, instead going into business with my dad, as a button salesman.

Every so often I think of old Lights and Paulie Beacon and Big Peter Capisce, with his way-too-big baseball bat, getting ready for nine hard-fought innings of two-on-two at our own Fenway Park. I'd do anything to grab my bat and glove and join them down at the Pit, but my pitching arm wouldn't last two innings. And I know Capisce—he'd make me pitch! But hey, even L.C. had to hang-em-up, I tell myself. Should be no shame in that, every superstar has to go down that road.

I pound the old leather on my Louie Cardinale glove. After all these years I still feel awful about lying to my father about my glove being stolen. He was so distraught, he bought me a replacement the next day, and I never, ever, washed it in the Cleanerama.

I can still see my name written next to L.C.'s and smell the leathery odor and baby oil. Did I ever tell you my father was the best dad in the world? I hope I remembered to tell him.

Well, with every passing spring training, another year of hope touches another generation of Sox fans. It's the out-of-control roller coaster we call Red Sox Nation, and nothing will change our minds about loving them.

I suppose you're wanting to know if we pulled it off. I'd like to think we did. But to be honest, a true hero never divulges his accomplishments, relying instead on what history says. The Red Sox did win the World Series in 2024. Would they have won without us? Perhaps, perhaps not.

There's no doubt some people would deplore what we did. Heck, even Robin Hood had his critics. And to our critics I say, you don't understand unless you're a true Red Sox fan.

ABOUT THE AUTHOR

A lifelong, fiercely partisan Boston Red Sox fan, Gerard Purciello spends quite a lot of time "waiting 'til next year," but he remains stubbornly optimistic. His poems and a short story were published in his college literary magazine, and he is at work on two other novels. Injured in an automobile accident when he was 18, Gerard is a paraplegic. If you'd like to write to him, his e-mail address is *GERARD2LO@AOL.COM.*

BROWN BARN BOOKS

Great books for great teens!
Adventure…romance…historical fiction…fantasy…

■ *The Secret Shelter*
By Sandi LeFaucheur
  Historical time travel to the 1940's and the WW II bombing of London. Can three teens find their way back to the 21st century?
ISBN: 0-974648140 $8.95/$12.75 Canada

■ *Idiot!*
By Colin Neenan
  Jim O'Reilly, 16, writes anonymous e-mail love letters to a high school gossip columnist and finds himself in People magazine, inadvertently famous and an unwilling national romantic hero.
ISBN: 0-974648116 $8.95/$12.75 Canada

■ *Running Horsemen*
By Dolph LeMoult
  Chance Bailey leaves Texas in search of his father in New York City, and falls in love with a wannabe Radio City Rockette, who happens to be the girlfriend of a jealous gangster.
ISBN: 0-974648108 $10.95/$15.95 Canada

continued on next page

■ *What's Happily Ever After Anyway?*
By Michelle Taylor
Miranda's fairy-tale romance collides with reality, touching the soul of every teen-age girl along the way. A must-have teen read.
ISBN: 0-974648132 $8.75/$12.75 Canada

■ *Home to the Sea*
By Chester Aaron
Hearing mysterious voices from the sea, rescuing a stranded whale, Marion discovers a family secret—is she really turning into a mermaid?
ISBN: 0-974648124 $8.75/$12.75 Canada

■ *Far From Burden Dell*
By Chris Coppel
Dognapped from her home in rural England, Amy, a Golden Retriever, is imprisoned in London and, escaping with five friends, must make her way through the perils of London to find her way home.
ISBN: 0-974648167 $8.95/$12.75 Canada

■ *Key to Aten*
By Lynn Sinclair
Jodi finds romance and danger in a strange alternative, warring world to which, although she doesn't know it, she alone has the key.
ISBN: 0-974648175 $8.95/$12.75 Canada

Available from your favorite bookseller or from the publisher.
Brown Barn Books
119 Kettle Creek Road
Weston CT 06883, U.S.A.
www.brownbarnbooks.com.